Jonathan's Journal

Ken Munro

GASLIGHT PUBLISHERS

 Gaslight Publishers
P.O. Box 258
Bird-In-Hand, PA 17505

Library of Congress Catalog Card Number 96-68076

ISBN Number   1-57087-244-9

Production design by Robin Ober
Professional Press
Chapel Hill, NC 27515-4371

Manufactured in the United States of America
99 98 97 96   10 9 8 7 6 5 4 3 2 1

Dedicated to
all my readers —
young and old,
who listen with
their imagination.

CHAPTER ONE

A short, strange shape slipped into the small country shop in the village of Bird-in-Hand. It slithered around the tourists, squeezed itself against a display case, and saluted. "Agent Brian Helm reporting in, sir. Shall we regroup upstairs in the debriefing room? Or should I blab out my findings right here in public?"

Sammy Wilson, 15, peered at his best friend, took a deep breath, and shook his head. "Brian, just tell me what you found out."

Brian shrugged. "Nothing. Not a thing. Zero. Zip."

"You were in the Bird-in-Hand Family Restaurant all morning and half of the afternoon and saw nothing suspicious?"

"Only tourists, locals, and waitresses with 'beanies' on their heads," replied Brian.

Sammy corrected his friend. "The young girls are called servers, not waitresses. And those 'beanies' they wear are ruffled cloth caps."

"What are you boys up to now?" asked Sammy's mother as she stepped out of the quilt room and joined her son behind the counter. Helen Wilson and her husband, Marc, ran the Bird-in-Hand Country Store. They sold Amish-made crafts to the millions of tourists that visited Lancaster County each year.

"We're working on a new case, Mrs. Wilson," said Brian proudly.

"There appears to be strange activity occurring at the restaurant," said Sammy. "Mr. John Smucker wants us to investigate."

Marc Wilson, standing at the cash register, handed a stuffed plastic bag to one of two smiling female tourists. The bag contained a neatly-folded Amish quilted wall hanging. "Thanks for stopping and have a nice day," he said, smiling back.

The woman holding the package hesitated. "Can you tell us where we can get something to eat?"

Mr. Wilson pointed. "The Bird-in-Hand Restaurant is right up the street past the farmer's market. A mile or so past that, on the left, is the Plain and Fancy Restaurant. And back this way," he pointed in the opposite direction, "if you turn left at the first traffic light, there's the Good 'N Plenty Restaurant."

After the tourists closed the door behind them, Mr. Wilson turned his attention to his son. "Now, what's this about strange happenings at the Bird-in-Hand Restaurant?" he asked.

"According to Mr. Smucker," said Sammy, "it's little things, like doors being left open when they should be closed. Puddles of water on the floor with no leaking pipes above. Furniture and objects rearranged. Strange noises."

"Sounds like ghosts to me," said Brian.

Mr. Wilson snickered.

Brian needed to prove his point. "Hey, this morning Mr. Smucker and I searched all through the restaurant, top and bottom, and saw nothing. And when you see nothing, you're seeing ghosts."

"Yeah, but ghosts don't eat," added Sammy.

"What?" said Brian.

"Didn't Mr. Smucker also say some food was missing?"

"Maybe ghosts do eat. They must get hungry from opening doors and moving furniture around. If I was a ghost in a restaurant, I sure would eat."

A group of tourists entered the shop followed by a man in a business suit. He was middle-aged with sandy hair combed straight back. The blue eyes behind the wire-rimmed glasses looked tired and troubled. He walked directly toward Sammy and Brian.

"Hello," said Sammy as he recognized Fred Barton from the television.

It was a sad situation. Fred's nineteen-year-old daughter had been missing for four days. She just disappeared from her aunt and uncle's store where she worked. The police suspected kidnapping but had turned up no clues or the girl. Fred appeared on television, pleading for her return.

"Sammy, Brian, may I talk with you in private? Detective Phillips said you boys might be able to help me." Fred glanced around and seemed uncomfortable as several more tourists entered the little shop.

"Let's go upstairs to my room," said Sammy. He led the way, squirming past the browsing tourists.

The young detective's bedroom was at the top and to the right of the narrow stairway that led up from the shop. First-time visitors were always overwhelmed by the variety of resources and equipment the room held. A wall-to-wall bookshelf displayed books of fiction and non-fiction. A small table held sophisticated crime lab equipment, assembled with the help of Detective Ben Phillips, a friend from the police department.

A large, old oak desk held a computer system and printer. A newly-enlarged bulletin board posted newspaper articles describing past cases Sammy and Brian had solved. The bulletin board was courtesy of Sammy's mother and father who wanted their son and Brian to know their work was appreciated by the public. They were also proud of the boys.

Fred Barton quickly got to the point. "Boys, my daughter, Karen, has been missing for four days now. I'm going out of my mind. She's my only daughter." He walked to the front window and looked down onto Main Street. "The police are doing all they can, but they have other cases, too." He turned from the window and faced the teenagers. "I need you boys to help me find her. Will you?"

Sammy saw the desperation in Mr. Barton's face. He knew the feeling. There were times in past cases when his friend's life had been threatened. "Yes, we'll help you find Karen," said Sammy.

"But we're already working a case now," said Brian. "Remember, the restaurant?"

"Yes, but that's just a small case. Ghosts, I think you said. *Right, Brian?*"

"Yeah, well, I guess we can handle two cases." Brian stood tall and proud. "Sure we can."

Sammy grabbed a spiral notebook and a pen and slid into his desk chair. "As I remember from what I read and heard, you, your wife, and daughter live in Lancaster. Your daughter was . . . is staying with her aunt and uncle down the street."

"Right. Kathy and Al Witmer," said Fred. "Kathy's my sister. Karen stays with them during the tourist season and works in their Bird-in-Hand Junction store." He returned to the window and glanced down to his left as if expecting to see his daughter standing in front of the Junction.

Brian backed up, collapsed on the bed, and stared at the ceiling. "So one day when Karen was working in the shop alone, she put a sign on the door, locked it, and never returned," he said, remembering what he had read in the newspapers.

Fred slipped into the nearby rocker and leaned forward, resting his elbows on his knees with his face in his hands. "That's right. Sounds strange, doesn't it?"

"What did the sign say?" asked Brian.

Fred uncovered his face, revealing the tears in his eyes. "Will return in five minutes. Five minutes."

"And that was four days ago," said Sammy to confirm the days of Karen's disappearance and to write it in his notebook. "And the police could find no reason for the note or for what happened to her?"

Mr. Barton shook his head. "It's real bizarre. You hear stories of other people going to the store for bread and never returning . . . but . . . And her car is still parked behind the shop. The police believe Karen might have been . . . abducted."

Sammy watched Mr. Barton and wondered why Karen stayed with her aunt and uncle when her home was only twenty minutes away in Lancaster. "Did Karen have any reason to run away?" asked Sammy. "Has she ever done it before?"

Fred Barton stood and paced the floor in front of the desk. "Once, five years ago, she ran away with a girlfriend. But it didn't last long. She was back in two days."

"Does she have a boyfriend?" asked Brian. "Maybe she ran away with him."

"Karen has a regular boyfriend. His name's Tom Killian. She's been dating him, on and off, for a year or so." Barton leaned on the desk and hesitated as Sammy's pencil scurried across the notebook. "Kathy told me a red-headed young man had been hanging around the store. Karen went on a date with him the day before she disappeared. We gave his name to the police. Scott Boyer, I think it is. He's from Philadelphia, here on vacation."

"I bet he's the redhead I saw here in the store yesterday," said Brian.

"They checked him out," said Barton. "The police say he's not involved with Karen's disappearance."

"Did anybody see Karen when she left the shop?" asked Sammy.

"Apparently not. The police checked around and found no witnesses."

Brian tried to visualize the scene as he focused on the ceiling. "Aren't tourists always coming in and out of the shop during the day? When would she be able to leave the shop without being seen?"

"One o'clock," said Sammy.

"What?" said Brian.

"One o'clock. That's when most tourists are eating lunch. There's hardly any traffic in our shop at that time."

"Maybe she was kidnapped," said Brian as he sprang up into a sitting position on the bed. "Somebody came into the shop, put a gun in her face, and made her leave with him in his car."

"And stopped to put a 'will-return-in-five-minutes' sign on the door," added Sammy sarcastically. Then he thought the better of it and added, "Was it your daughter's handwriting on the sign?"

"That's the strange part. The sign was printed in heavy block letters. Like someone under stress. That's what the police said anyway. But we can't be sure that it's not Karen's handwriting."

"So she either left the shop on her own or was taken by someone," said Brian.

"What did her aunt and uncle think of her new boyfriend—" Sammy glanced down at his notes. "Scott Boyer?" asked Sammy.

"I heard them tell the police that he was a nice enough guy," said Fred Barton. "She's nineteen and on her own. She makes her own decisions. I have to believe she's out there somewhere, and she's all right." He moved to the window to hide the tears and to once again search the street below for his daughter.

Sammy poised his pencil on the note pad. "Can you give us some names of her friends?"

"I can think of only one more. She has a girlfriend, Andrea Hill. Works up at the restaurant. She's been to the house several times. Lives in this area somewhere. We gave these names to the police, but I'm hoping her friends will reveal more to you than to the police. Please find her for me," he pleaded. "There's so much I haven't said to her."

Before the boys could answer, Barton looked at his watch. "I must go. I have a funeral to attend in Lancaster." He placed his business card on the desk next to the computer and left the room.

As the narrow stairway echoed Mr. Barton's departure, Brian raced for the card left by their new client. Sammy beat him to it.

"Well, what does it say? What business is he in? Where does he live?" Brian blurted out as he rushed to stand behind his friend.

Sammy held the card for them both to see. "Well, what about that? Our Mr. Barton is a funeral director in Lancaster."

Brian smiled, put his hands on Sammy's shoulders, and squeezed. "We can be sure of one thing when he gets home."

"What's that?" asked Sammy.

"Mr. Barton won't find an empty coffin displaying a sign, 'Will return in five minutes.'"

CHAPTER TWO

Fifteen minutes later Sammy hung up the phone, flipped over two pages of notes, and tossed the pad aside. "According to our friend, Detective Ben Phillips, the police still have no leads in the case. No one saw Karen, and no one knows why she would want to run away. And Mr. Barton was right. The police are assuming she was abducted."

"But the sign on the door," said Brian.

"They believe someone else wrote it."

Brian by this time was comfortably lying in his usual position on the bed, staring at the ceiling in deep thought. "You know, it's possible Karen saw something or someone outside and hurriedly printed the sign, intending to return in five minutes. Instead she was seized and taken away."

"With all the tourists roaming Main Street, someone surely would have seen something."

"Yeah, well, tourists are here today, gone tomorrow. Any possible witnesses would have been gone before the police even knew she was missing."

"Yes, you could be right," said Sammy.

Brian locked his hands together behind his head and smiled at the ceiling.

"Detective Phillips gave me a list of Karen's friends and where we can reach them. He suggested the same as Mr. Barton, that we should have a talk with her friends. They might tell us something they didn't tell the police. How about you doing some interviewing tomorrow? Here's a list of their names, addresses, and phone numbers."

As Brian pictured himself in the role of interrogator, he slipped from the bed, grabbed the list, and strolled to the front window. His eyes followed a stream of tourists as they meandered in and out of shops along the narrow village street. Main Street was also known as the Old Philadelphia Pike and Route 340 and traveled right through the heart of Amish country.

Across the street and to the right, stood the Village Inn of Bird-in-Hand. The inn was believed to be as old as the Old Philadelphia Pike itself. The original inn had been a crude log hut. But restored in 1852, after a fire the previous year, the building was now a three-story, eleven-room, Victorian inn.

A young man was leaning against one of the four columns in front of the inn. He was watching the activity around the Bird-in-Hand Country Store. His red hair glistened in the afternoon sunlight, as his eyes drifted up to the bedroom window.

Brian's eyes locked on those of the young man. A chill ran through his body. He felt guilty. Like he was caught spying on the unsuspecting tourists. Brian backed away from the window, hesitated, and took another look at the figure on the porch. His eyes squinted as he leaned closer. He had seen that person before.

Detecting Brian's strange motions, Sammy asked, "What's wrong?"

Brian waved his hand. "The fellow over there on the porch of the inn. He's looking over here. I think that's Scott Boyer."

Leaving his notes at his desk, Sammy crossed to the window. "Well, he has red hair. Let's go." He grabbed his pad and pen as he rushed past the desk. "If it is him, we can ask him some questions about Karen. If we can talk to him now, that's one name off your list."

The two teenage detectives hurried as they maneuvered around the tourists and dodged the cars. When they arrived safely on the other side of Main Street, their target was still in sight.

As the boys suddenly materialized in front of the young man, he recoiled. The twenty-year-old redhead, wearing a T-shirt, jeans, and sneakers, appeared shy and embarrassed. "Hi, you're Sammy and Brian aren't you? I was just coming to see you. I'm Scott Boyer."

"What did you want with us?" asked Brian suspiciously.

"It's a private matter. I don't want to talk about it here. Let's go up to my room." With that he turned and disappeared around the side of the inn.

Sammy and Brian looked at each other and shrugged. Curiosity prompted Sammy to follow the young man. Habit prompted Brian to follow Sammy. Both boys were also anxious to see the inside of this famous local inn. Scott Boyer was their ticket inside.

The redhead was waiting for them at the opened side door which was the entrance to the inn. The young detectives entered and were surprised to find themselves in what looked like a barroom.

"Well, if it isn't Sammy and Brian, Bird-in-Hand's great detectives," said a voice from behind the bar.

The boys quickly recovered as they recognized the two figures standing at the bar. "Hello, Mr. and Mrs. Young," said Sammy while Brian savored the words "Bird-in-Hand's great detectives."

Richmond and Janice Young were the inn-keepers. The previous year they had discussed the fascinating history of the inn in Sammy's and Brian's history class.

"Your check-in counter looks like a bar," said Brian.

Richmond slipped out from behind the massive piece of solid wood. "This is most of the original bar," he stated proudly. "The bar, even the backdrop with the mirror, was moved from the room next to this one." He pointed to the southeast corner of the building.

"Wasn't this originally a one-story stagecoach stop back in the 1700's?" asked Sammy.

"Yes, that's right," answered Janice.

"Can I see you boys upstairs now?" asked Scott Boyer who didn't seem the least bit interested in the conversation. He headed down the hallway and up the stairs.

The boys said good-bye to the innkeepers and hurried after the redhead. Seeing no one on the second floor, they continued to the top landing. Scott was waiting for them at an opened door labeled the Bousman Room.

Inside, the Victorian room appeared luxurious. Scott sat on the edge of the double bed and motioned for the boys to sit in the two chairs by a small table. "I need your help. I can't do this by myself."

Sammy tried to anticipate what was coming. Was Scott also trying to enlist their help in finding Karen? He had dated the young girl, and maybe he, too, was concerned for her safety. "What is it you can't do by yourself?" he asked.

The young redhead leaned forward and said, "Recover a jeweled necklace worth one million dollars."

Chapter Three

While the boys were recovering from shock, Scott reached into his suitcase and carefully displayed several pieces of worn, very brittle paper. He separated the papers and placed them gently on the bed. "I have copies of these, but I wanted you to see the originals."

Both boys jumped to their feet and approached the display. They looked down at the pages spread across the quilt. The old, sepia-colored manuscript looked at home on the Victorian bed.

Sammy scanned the mysterious papers. He remained quiet as he read and tried to make sense of it all. Here was a very young man who had been in town for a short time, lived in an historic inn, dated a girl who is presently missing, and now displays papers that has some connection to a valuable necklace. Sammy was eager to know more. "From what I can make out of the writing, these are pages of an old diary. Are they?"

"They are pages from a journal written by an ancestor of mine, Jonathan Boyer. Here, look, it's dated April 25, 1792."

"Wow! That's old," said Brian.

"Where did you get it?" asked Sammy.

"I was helping my grandmother clear out the attic—"

"In Philadelphia?" asked Brian.

"Yeah, I found an old suitcase with a tag tied to the handle. The tag was dated May 2, 1792, with the words 'Return to Mrs. Mildred Boyer,' and it had the address of that house. I showed it to my grandma, and she said she wasn't aware the suitcase was there. The house had been in the family for generations. Grandma said each generation probably just threw their junk up in the attic."

"Well, that answers the question, What did people do with their junk before garage sales?" said Brian.

"Grandma wanted me to throw it away, but I opened it and looked inside. There were some moldy clothes and an old notebook that fell apart when I touched it. I started reading and came to the part about a priceless necklace that Jonathan was taking to Lancaster to sell."

"But that was so long ago," said Brian. "What does it have to do with now?"

"Read it for yourself. Then you'll know why I'm here, and why I'm asking for your help."

Sammy and Brian carefully read the two-hundred-dred-year-old message.

April 23, 1792

Left Philadelphia in good spirits. My mood soon changed. The road is so bad I fear the trip now. If I had no need of financial resources, I would leave the coach today. But, alas, I must continue the trip. The jewels I must keep hidden for fear of robbers. Stopped at the old Oak Inn for the night. It is good to get out of the rain.

April 24, 1792

No sign of rain. The day is pleasant enough but mud has caused great ruts. I fear for the horses. The six horses travel slowly today and thus so the coach. It is imperative I not be late for the auction for my prize is the main attraction. There are six of us in the coach. The others watch and wonder what I write.

April 25, 1792

Our driver is mindless. Today he drove upon a large stump which stood in our way. We were thrown out of our seats a considerable distance. I received no hurt. A man follows on horseback. I must stay alert lest he is after my gold necklace. The jewels will sleep with me tonight.

April 28, 1792

How much longer must I endure this trip? We are drawing near to Lancaster. Thank God the misery will soon be over. We arrive in Lancaster tomorrow. I still have much to fear — The man on horseback still trails us. I wonder why he follows? These secret auctions bring out the criminal element. I must abandon my love of Indian jewelry. Henceforth the curse belongs to the buyer. The night grows dark. We disembark at the Bird-in-Hand Inn. I am being watched. The stranger has acquired the room next to mine. I suspect my life is in danger.

10:05 P.M.

I must record here now what transpired tonight. Upon arriving and setting my things aside in my room, I requested a shovel from the innkeeper. I walked a considerable distance in the darkness making sure I was not followed. I then unhappily fed my necklace to the ground. I then returned immediately to the inn. I can now retire knowing my necklace is safe. I will reclaim my prize in the morning.

60
M to P
X 6 to L

"I've been trying for a week to make sense out of this jumbled mess, 60 M to P X 6 to L. I believe it's a clue to where he buried the necklace. What do you think? I heard you boys are good at solving puzzles."

Sammy's blue eyes sparkled as they took in the mixture of numbers and letters, "Seems he constructed a code so he wouldn't forget where he buried his treasure."

"What makes you think the necklace is still where he put it?" asked Brian.

Sammy, wanting to strengthen Brian's detection skills, asked his friend, "What date did Scott say was on the tag tied to Jonathan Boyer's suitcase?"

"May 2, 1792."

"And what's written after the strange arrangement of numerals and letters?"

"Nothing."

Sammy glanced at Scott and said, "I assume there were blank pages after this one."

Scott shook his head and smiled, realizing Sammy had picked up on the clues.

Brian smiled. "Jonathan didn't have any more entries because he was dead. So the stranger did killed him, and several days later his baggage was returned to his widow. Right, Sammy?"

"Probably along with the body," said Scott. "My Grandma recalled hearing about a distant relative being murdered near Lancaster."

"Even so, what makes you think the necklace is still in the ground?" asked Brian.

"I figured it this way. If the stranger followed and saw Jonathan bury the necklace, he would wait, dig it up, and be on his way, leaving Jonathan alive. That leaves one other possibility which makes sense."

"You mean," said Sammy, "sometime after Jonathan made the last notations in his journal, the book was put away. The stranger slipped into his room and confronted him. He demanded the necklace. Jonathan wouldn't tell. He pulled a gun or a knife and threatened him. Jonathan still refused to give up the necklace. In frustration or in a struggle, the stranger used the gun or the knife and killed Jonathan. The killer then quickly escaped without the necklace."

"That's the way I see it," said Scott.

"There's one other possible ending to your story, Sammy," said Brian. "Jonathan is scared. He hands over the journal with directions to the buried necklace. The stranger now has what he came for, so he kills Jonathan." Brian shrugged and added, "End of story, end of necklace."

Sammy smiled. "Are you saying the killer took the journal with him?"

"Well, no, but . . . He wrote the directions on another piece of paper."

"Brian, if you were the killer which would you do? Take time to write down the directions or rip out the page and take it with you?"

"Okay, you're right. He didn't get the directions, so he didn't get the necklace," said Brian reluctantly. Nevertheless he wasn't about to give up. "Okay, how's this ending to the story? Jonathan is killed, the stranger is unable to find the necklace, and the necklace remains in the ground." He then added dramatically, "*The Indian curse strikes again.*"

Scott glanced down at the journal pages. "It does mention a curse."

Sammy reflected inwardly. Although curses were referred to in books he had read, he wasn't ready to accept that idea. But he would keep an open mind. He shrugged to indicate to the others that it was a possibility.

The papers Scott pulled from his suitcase were copies of the originals still lying on the bed. He held the duplicates in front of the teenage detectives. "I tried to make sense out of Jonathan's code, and I can't. Will you help me solve the puzzle?"

The dangling papers drew Sammy like a magnet. He was starving for a challenging puzzle. Even if the necklace was long gone, the satisfaction of delving into the eighteenth century was enough to whet his appetite. Here was a two-hundred-year-old treasure map being handed to him. How could he refuse?

Sammy looked at Brian. Brian looked at Sammy. "Okay, we'll take the case," said Sammy as he reached for the copies.

Scott released his grip on the papers. "What do you charge for your work? I don't have much money now, but when we find the—"

"We don't charge," interrupted Sammy.

"Yeah, we do it for the experience. Right, Sammy?" said Brian with a sour face.

"Hey," said Scott, "when the necklace is found and sold, you boys will get a nice hunk of money."

Brian's hazel eyes sparkled. "Oh, that's gr—"

"No, we couldn't accept it," returned Sammy. "We only ask for money to cover expenses."

"We can't be rude, Sammy," said Brian, jumping in. "He'll probably force us to take it. Right, Scott?"

"Absolutely," said Scott.

"There, you see?" said Brian triumphantly.

Sammy cast his partner a cold look. "We'll talk about this later, *Brian*."

"Look, I haven't told anybody about this. Only my grandmother knows about the journal. She promised me she wouldn't mention it to anyone. You must keep this a secret. Don't let anyone get his or her hands on that information. I don't want to end up like Jonathan."

A cracking noise jolted the trio from their vows of secrecy.

Their heads turned.

A rustling noise sounded from beyond the door.

Faint footsteps followed in the hall.

Someone had been listening at the door!

Chapter Four

"What's that?" whispered Scott.

Sammy put his finger to his lips. "Shhh," he whispered and crept to the door. He listened, putting his ear to the wood. Hearing nothing, he flung open the door.

"Be careful," shouted Brian in a whisper.

Sammy saw no one in the short hall. He rushed to the stairs and peered down. A man, walking slowly, had turned from the stairway on the second floor. He had a beard and mustache, was in his fifties, heavy-set, and dressed as a typical tourist. Sammy had trained himself to observe details. The man wore a multi-colored shirt, shorts, and baseball cap. His thin legs carried him down the next set of stairs to the first floor.

Since Sammy couldn't prove anything if he stopped the tourist, he decided to follow him. On the first floor the man walked through the hallway to the check-in counter. The young detective watched as the man spoke briefly with Richmond Young, turned, and then left the inn.

By this time Sammy had some anxious company gathered around him.

"What happened?" asked Scott.

"Who was it?" asked Brian.

"Let's find out," said Sammy as he led them to the counter.

"Well, boys, how do you like our old inn?" asked Richmond.

"It's great," said Sammy. "Say, I thought I recognized the man who just left. Is he someone famous?"

Richmond gave Sammy an odd look. "I don't think so. He's a tourist from Arizona, Robert Turner. He has a room on the third floor, next to yours, Mr. Boyer."

Brian flopped back on the bed, allowing his feet to dangle over the edge. His eyes focused on the ceiling. Sammy made himself comfortable at his desk and observed his partner. The boys had just returned from across the street and had some planning to do. Without even trying, the Sammy and Brian detective team had three cases to solve.

"Wow!" said Brian, his eyes roaming the ceiling, "three cases. If this keeps up, we'll have to expand our business. We can get Joyce Myers to help us again." Joyce had helped the boys solve their last case, *Amish Justice*. "Hey, we could even open a branch office in Lancaster. Right, Sammy?"

"Oh, so you want Joyce to help us again." Sammy couldn't resist the dig. "You like her, do you?"

"Yeah, she's all right. She's more fun than you are. You should loosen up a little, you know." Brian's eyes continued to scan the ceiling.

"Are you looking for your friend?" asked Sammy, glancing up to help his partner with the search.

"What?" said Brian.

"Are you searching for your spider friend on the ceiling?"

"He's not really my friend. He's just an associate." Brian maintained a serious face as he went into his act.

"Sorry," said Sammy. "Do you see him?"

"Larry."

"What?"

"Larry. His name is Larry," answered Brian with a hint of a smile.

"That's strange. Last week you told me his name was Walter."

"Yeah, well, Walter is his police undercover name."

"So Larry the spider is a policeman is he? Here I thought he was a baseball player."

"What gave you that idea?"

"Someone told me he catches flies."

Moaning, Brian lifted his head from the bed and looked at Sammy. "When I said for you to loosen up, I didn't mean for you to fall apart."

The grin on Sammy's face indicated he enjoyed beating his best friend at his own game.

"Okay, okay, you win," said Brian, realizing Sammy was proving a point. "I was wrong. You're more fun when you're serious."

Sammy picked up his note pad. "Good, then let's get back to work. First, the Bird-in-Hand Family Restaurant case. You reported that you detected nothing out of the ordinary happening at the restaurant today."

"Right." Brian's head rested on the bed again as he refocused on the ceiling. "Mr. Smucker and I checked all the dining rooms, both upstairs and downstairs. We examined the equipment, and talked with the workers. We didn't turn up a clue."

"Okay, let's put that aside for awhile. I suggest we contact the restaurant in two or three days to check if any more ghost-like activities have occurred. If they do, Brian, you and I will spend a night in the restaurant, alone."

"Alone with the ghosts," added Brian.

Sammy ignored the comment and continued. "Case two, finding Karen." He glanced at his notes. "According to what Scott Boyer just told us before we left him, he dated Karen once, the day before she disappeared. He said Karen appeared normal. And he had a date to see her again the same day she had disappeared."

Brian sat up on the bed. "How can Scott take time for girls when he's trying to find a million-dollar necklace?" Brian shook his head. "And he said he didn't know anything about her disappearance. Doesn't it seem strange that the trouble at the restaurant *and* Karen's disappearance happened just after Scott Boyer came to town? After we help him find the necklace, we might disappear, too. Right, Sammy?"

"What reason would he have for making us disappear?"

"Well, with a necklace worth a million dollars, anything can happen. And we'll be in the middle of it. I say we better be careful." Brian began pacing around the room.

Sammy reconsidered and nodded in agreement. "You're right, Brian. With a million dollars at stake, we do have to be careful."

Brian grinned and added dramatically, "Yes, now that we're well-known all over Lancaster County, we are bombarded with new cases. We are celebrities. Fans line up to get our autographs. People seek out our services, day and night. We put our lives on the line every day. And for what? For what? I ask you. Do we seek money or fame? No. All we want is—"

Brian's dramatic presentation brought him to the table near the door. He looked down and saw an envelope addressed to Sammy. He picked it up and continued, "All we want are letters like this one, thanking us for a job well done." He shook his head as he brushed his fingers through his hair. "Probably another girl asking for a lock of my curly hair," he said and presented the unopened envelope to his friend.

Sammy rolled his eyes and shook his head. "Brian, you're crazy. Harmless, but crazy." He glanced at the envelope. It was addressed to him all right and with no return address. "Hey, I didn't know this letter was over there."

"Well, open it," said Brian seriously.

Sammy read it and his face went blank. He flipped the paper for Brian to read. It wasn't a letter. It was a warning, written in block letters: STAY AWAY FROM SCOTT BOYER AND THE NECKLACE OR YOU WILL BE SORRY.

CHAPTER FIVE

S ammy called down the stairway to his father. "When did this letter come for me?"

"In the morning mail," said Mr. Wilson. "I put in on your table when you were in the bathroom this morning. Sorry, I forgot to tell you. Anything wrong?"

The young detective hesitated. He didn't want to alarm his parents. "No, it's all right. Thank you."

"Who would want us to stay away from Scott? and why?" asked Sammy.

"It's the curse!" said Brian. The serious tone of his voice contrasted his earlier theatrical comedy.

"A curse can't write and mail a letter," said Sammy. "What do you think the 'you will be sorry' part means?"

"It means if we continue to mess with this case, we'll have a curse put on us."

Sammy smiled. "Maybe on you, but not on me."

"Yeah, what makes you immune to curses?"

"Knowledge," said Sammy. "Knowledge overrides curses."

The more Brian thought about that, the less he wanted to pursue the matter. He was always eager to learn from his best friend. There were times when he made light of Sammy's lectures, but he realized his friend was trying to impart some wisdom. "Yeah, we're too smart to fall for that junk. Right, Sammy?"

Sammy resettled into his chair and combed his fingers through his straight black hair. His somber blue eyes shifted from his friend to the note. "Brian, whoever sent this letter knows about the necklace. We need to do some brainstorming."

Brainstorming was a method the boys used to kick around ideas to solve problems. They would start with a question. The answer to that question led to other questions. When the exchange of ideas was productive, it opened up new paths of investigation.

"Okay, why would someone not want us to help Scott find the necklace?" asked Brian.

"Maybe he or she wants the necklace for himself or herself." Sammy leaned forward and picked up the copy of the last journal page. He gazed at the mysterious directions to the hidden necklace. "But, Scott's grandmother kept quiet about the journal. Scott certainly kept it a secret. How would anyone else know about it?"

Brian stood behind Sammy and gazed at the puzzle. "I know! The man at the inn, Robert Turner.

You know, the tourist from Arizona. He was listening at the door."

Sammy examined the envelope again. "That happened today. According to the postmark, this envelope was mailed to me yesterday."

"Maybe he broke into Scott's room several days ago and read the journal."

"How would he know to do that? Turner didn't know about the journal," said Sammy.

Brian became quite animated and said, "Let's say Turner was a thief. He broke into the room, accidentally stumbled across the journal, read it, and made a copy of the puzzle."

Sammy continued the thought for Brian but less dramatically. "Turner tries to solve the puzzle which we think reveals where Jonathan hid the necklace. He can't figure it out. Today he sees us going into Scott's room. He listens at the door and hears that we are going to help solve the puzzle." Sammy pointed to the paper. "So *yesterday* he sends this warning to scare us off, giving him more time to discover the necklace's location and dig it up."

"I see what's wrong with that idea," said Brian. "Mr. Turner didn't know until today that we were involved in this case. And the note was mailed yesterday. But that doesn't make sense. Nobody knew we would be on this case yesterday, not even us."

"Only one person could know," said Sammy. "Scott Boyer."

"Right," said Brian. "But why would he warn us to stay away from himself if he wants us to help him. It doesn't make sense."

Sammy had ways of dealing with dead ends. He would attack this one from another approach. He quickly swept his hand across his desk, pushing the papers aside. All but one sheet. The most fascinating and important writing of all remained before them:

60

M TO P

X 6 TO L

"We must solve this puzzle as soon as possible," said Sammy. "Look for patterns, special groupings of the numerals and letters. For instance, why does the sixty stand by itself at the top? Why is the M to P grouped together followed by X six to L?"

"Yeah, if I wrote directions, I would write them on one line if there was room."

"Sixty. M to P," said Sammy slowly. "Times six to L. Sounds like directions in a game. Sixty moves to P times six to L. Mean anything to you?"

"No, but the M could be a measurement." For some reason the inside back cover of his sixth-grade math book came to mind. Brian smiled. "Meters. Sixty meters to . . . What word starts with P that could be a marker?"

Sammy's head started spinning. He saw where this mental exercise was leading. "Post, pipe, pole . . . Brian, solving this puzzle is going to be a challenge. Do you see how worthless these directions are going to be after two hundred years?"

Brian walked to the front window. He eyed the Village Inn as it was today. He saw the houses and shops that now lined the Old Philadelphia Pike. The road, once dirt and mud and bounded by trees and fields, was now paved and swarming with modern vehicles and tourists.

His hazel eyes were sad as he turned from the window. "Yeah, the markers will be gone. We missed them by about two hundred years."

CHAPTER SIX

Later that night on the third floor of the Village Inn, a man scratched his bearded chin. He shifted his position again for the third time in the last five minutes. It wasn't the bed. The bed was comfortable enough. It wasn't the sound of Amish buggies sharing the road outside his window with late-night tourists either. It was the waiting. Waiting. Waiting for the necklace to be found.

Further up and across the street, the Bird-in-Hand Family Restaurant sat dark and quiet. The stillness was the rest it deserved after a busy day. Suddenly, in the lower level, a silhouette emerged from a small enclosure and moved behind a small flashlight. The individual's routine was the same as in previous nights. It was critical that this person's enterprise remained a secret. The lives of two people depended on it.

Around 9:30 the next morning, Brian was sitting on a bench in the Park City Mall. His father had dropped him off, but he would have to take the bus home. He had never questioned anyone on a bench before. First on his list of "interviewees" was Karen Barton's boyfriend, Tom Killian. Brian had called him the previous evening. Tom agreed to meet Brian at the mall in the morning before he went to work at Sears.

Brian had it all figured out. Tom had been Karen's boyfriend for several years. Then Scott Boyer comes into the picture. Tom gets jealous and confronts Karen. He wants to know where he stands. Karen says he doesn't. Tom gets angry and . . . Karen is now among the missing. So now Brian was ready for Tom Killian. Yep, he was ready.

"You Brian Helm?" said the unexpected voice from behind the bench.

The scared teenage detective jumped and jerked his body to his left. All of his rehearsed questions and strategies vanished into the air. "Yeah, I'm Brian Helm," he heard himself say.

The tall young man rounded the bench and flopped down next to Brian. He folded his arms across his chest and stared up into space. "I'm Tom Killian. You told me on the phone that you and Sammy Wilson were hired by Karen's father to find her. I hope you do. But as I said, I already told the police all I know." Tom Killian's lap vanished as he stretched out straight and stiff. Brian thought he was going to slide right off the bench onto the floor.

Something about this guy's appearance scared the young detective. His long brown hair was pulled back into a ponytail. His eyes were tight narrow slits as though straining in a tug-of-war with his hair. A small gold ring pierced his left ear. A black sport shirt and black jeans hung from his thin body. A scant mustache was trying to make him look older than his twenty years. It didn't.

Brian pulled out his notebook and pen and glanced at his questions. "Were you still dating Karen before she disappeared?"

"Yes," he answered sharply.

Brian noted his reply in the space after the question. He glanced at the next question. "Did Karen ever date anyone else?"

Tom came out of his trance, his lap returned, and he glared at Brian for the first time. "Yes, she dated somebody. But you already know that. And you know his name. It's Scott Boyer. So how about asking me some questions you don't have the answers to."

Wow! I have a hostile witness here, thought Brian. And smart, too. Brian went straight for the question he had underlined. The question he thought Sammy would be proud of. "When Karen was killed, were you here at work or someplace else."

"I was . . . I mean . . . Did you say killed? Is Karen dead?"

At that moment Brian tried to read Tom's reaction. Was it a genuine response to the mention of

Karen's death or was it play-acting? Did Tom know she was dead because he had killed her?

"Oh, no, no, no," said Brian, "I meant to say, When Karen *disappeared*, where were you?" Brian was looking down at his notes to hide any trace of deception his eyes might reveal.

Tom answered the question. "I was home in Lancaster. The police checked. A neighbor saw me park my car and go into the house at the time the sign was posted on the shop door." Tom peeked at his watch, stood up, and headed for Sears. He turned around and slowly walked backwards. "Look, I think she just ran away for a while. She's done it before."

"Why did she run away before?" asked Brian.

"He forced her to run away."

"Who?"

As he turned and hurried to work, Tom's voice shot back. "Her father."

CHAPTER SEVEN

While Brian was on his way to the Bird-in-Hand Family Restaurant for his second interview, something was disturbing Sammy. It was a comment made by Brian the previous day. He had said the mysterious happenings at the restaurant, Karen Barton's disappearance, and the possibility of buried jewelry, all began with the arrival of Scott Boyer.

Was Scott Boyer responsible for Karen's disappearance? Or were others involved? Sammy wondered. Copies were made of the journal, Scott had said. Who made the copies? Where were the copies made? Did the excitement of finding the journal cause Scott to talk too loosely among his friends? Was he followed here to the Village Inn as Jonathan had been?

After Brian went home the night before, Sammy read the journal pages again. He made a list of clues to help him understand Jonathan's trip to Lan-

caster. This was the list he now took from his desk
drawer:

Clues from Journal

1. urgent need of money
2. had jewels
3. going to an auction
4. "my prize is main attraction"
5. auction is secret
6. bring out criminal element
7. love of Indian artifacts
8. a curse?
9. followed by man on horse
10. man in room next door
11. got a shovel
12. went out in darkness
13. walked a considerable distance
14. necklace put into ground
15. necklace made up of jewels?

Sammy read through the clues again. He
strongly suspected that what Jonathan was taking
to Lancaster was an Indian necklace containing jewels. It was reasonable to assume the necklace might
be very valuable, since it was to be the highlight of
the auction.

Now the auction itself. A secret auction that
brings out the criminal element? Sammy wondered
about that. Did it mean the collectors themselves
were criminals? Sammy wasn't sure, but he had
read enough books to know smuggled or stolen

artifacts were bought by unscrupulous collectors. Was that the case here? Maybe the necklace, originally stolen, was from Jonathan's private collection. Or was this simply an auction advertised only to collectors to keep out the riffraff?

Sammy took Jonathan's puzzle and examined it again. He had never seen a puzzle in this form before. Evidently the position of the numbers and letters were important. Sixty stands alone. Was sixty a number on a building? he wondered. But Jonathan went out in the blackness of the night. The journal mentions nothing about a lantern. How could he see anything? Moonlight. Yeah, there had to be some moonlight.

Sammy glanced at number thirteen on his list of clues from the journal. He shook his head. "Why would he walk a considerable distance?" he said aloud to the bedroom walls. "Why go out into the dark at all, especially if you suspect you're going to be mugged?" He waited, but the bedroom walls didn't answer his questions. He missed Brian.

Brainstorming was more fun with his friend. "That's easy to answer," Brian would say. "He snuck out into the darkness so he wouldn't be seen. Right, Sammy?" Sammy smiled at the imagined response. He gathered the papers, placed them back into the desk drawer, and headed for the restaurant.

Brian had two objectives in mind when he hopped onto the padded swivel chair at the counter. He was going to question Andrea Hill, Karen Barton's friend, who worked here at the restaurant. And he was going to be on the lookout for ghosts. The force of his attack on the moving seat, however, caused him to overshoot his mark. He ended up facing the Amishman sitting to his right. The look Brian got from the Amishman told him the Amishman wasn't expecting company for lunch.

"Having trouble?" asked a pretty, young girl as Brian wiggled his way to face front.

Brian was embarrassed but he recovered quickly. "Oh, I just got my learner's permit. I'm not used to these automatic swivel chairs yet. You know how chairs are. Each one handles a little differently," he said and grinned.

The young waitress smiled back. Her name tag read "Andrea," which was the reason Brian had picked that seat. Andrea wore a white outfit with a red-colored ruffled cap and apron. "Do you want something to drink?" she asked as she handed him a menu.

Brian went into his secret agent routine as he leaned in close and whispered. "I'm Brian Helm. I called you yesterday."

"Oh, yes." She gave him a look of recognition and said, "You're the detective who rides a bicycle. I see you and Sammy riding around town."

The word "bicycle" somehow shattered Brian's image of himself as a secret agent. "Hey, I know you're busy, but we're trying to find Karen."

"I'll take a break in a couple of minutes." She pointed toward the cashier. "Wait for me over there on the benches."

Brian nodded and slowly swiveled and slipped from the stool, leaving it in neutral. He smiled to himself, satisfied with his flawless dismount.

Guests were being escorted into the main dining area as Brian took a seat on the bench. Other tourists were picking up and examining merchandise from a display area nearby. Books detailing Amish life shared a metal wire rack with books on quilts and quilting.

Five minutes later, Andrea came around the cashier counter and sat next to Brian. "What can I do to help you find Karen? I already told the police that she must have been taken by somebody. Grabbed and kidnapped. It happens all the time. She's dead by now. I just know it."

Brian whipped out the small pad and pen from his pocket. The pen rambled across the notebook recording Andrea's hideous remarks. How could these ugly thoughts come from such a pretty face? wondered Brian. What kind of friend would even consider such ideas? No hint of hope or caring showed on Andrea's face.

"How long have you two been friends?"

"Three years. I met her when she first came to work in the shop owned by her aunt and uncle."

"Karen lived in Lancaster and you lived here. How did that work?"

"Well, she was here in the summers. And she . . . she didn't like to be home. She didn't like her parents too much, especially her father."

Ah, thought Brian, there it was again. Her father. He held his breath and hoped. "Do you know why she didn't like her father?"

"Yeah, he made her help him in the embalming room. She hated it."

Brian cringed and starred that entry in his notes. "Where were you when Karen disappeared?"

"Right here at work."

That will be easy to check, thought Brian. "What do you know about Karen's boyfriend, Tom Killian?"

"He's okay, I guess," said Andrea. "Anyway, Karen stopped dating him. She's not much for boyfriends right now. You can't trust them. When Karen comes back . . . she . . . she . . ."

When Karen comes back, thought Brian. He wrote down every word. For a girl who earlier had a death wish for Karen, she certainly had changed her tune fast.

"So you think Karen *will* be back?"

"No, she won't," Andrea said quickly. "She's never coming back. I just meant if there is a possibility of . . ."

"Do you know of any reason for Karen to run away?"

Andrea glanced toward the counter area. "No. Hey, I have to go now. I must get back on duty. Maybe we can talk another time." With that she left the bench, rounded the cashier counter, and was gone.

Please find her. I hope the police find Karen. She's a decent girl. Do what you can to find her. These were the words that were never said by Andrea. Strange, thought Brian.

"Get anything we can use from your interviews?" asked Sammy, who suddenly appeared on the bench next to Brian.

Brian closed his spiral notebook. "Yeah, lots of good stuff from Tom and Andrea." Brian peered right and left as though foreign spies were lurking about. "I'd rather not talk about it here. Let's go back to headquarters."

"Pretty secret stuff, huh?" said Sammy. He held up a paper folded in half. "What about this? If you're being so secretive, why did I just find this note lying carelessly on your bike seat? It's addressed to you and me. Who gave it to you?"

"Hey, I don't know anything about it. It was on my bike? What's it say?" asked Brian as he abandoned his secret agent mode.

"Here, read it."

Brian held the unfolded paper close and read the printed note. STAY AWAY FROM SCOTT BOYER. BEWARE. HE IS DANGEROUS. Brian looked at Sammy. "And this was sitting on my bike?"

Sammy nodded. "Yep."

"Then it was put there while I've been in here."

"It could be anybody, someone from the restaurant or from outside," said Sammy. "But one thing seems clear. The notes are not threats. They are warnings."

"What do you mean?" asked Brian, handing the paper back to Sammy.

"I think someone is trying to tell us something." Suddenly Sammy's blue eyes flashed to the food counter. "Look, someone's trying to get our attention."

"Who?" asked Brian.

"Scott Boyer."

Scott was smiling and waving the teenage detectives over his way.

Sammy slipped the note into his pocket and leaned toward Brian. "Let's go, but don't mention the note."

"Have you eaten yet?" asked Scott as the boys approached. "I would like to buy two hard-working detectives lunch. Come on. I saved two seats for you."

The teenagers said nothing as they joined Scott at the counter. But they were thinking plenty. Sammy took a side glance at their client. Could Scott really be a threat? he wondered. Why did Scott always seem to be present when things happened? Like now with the note on the bike.

Brian eased gently onto the padded swivel seat and flashed a victory smile at the girl who handed him the menu. He had plenty to wonder about, too. Like, do they serve hot dogs and sauerkraut here?

If they do, will they serve the sauerkraut on the side? "I'll have a hot dog with sauerkraut," he said, his face retaining the smile.

"Sorry, today's not sauerkraut day. Only on days we have sauerkraut platters, do we have it for hot dogs."

That bit of news wiped the smile from Brian's face. He looked to Sammy and shrugged.

"Brian, now is the time to venture into new territory," said Sammy, allowing his blue eyes to lock onto the server's brown eyes. "I'll have a hamburger with mustard and onions."

"Right, okay," said Brian as he glanced at the name badge. "Okay, Jenny, give me a hamburger with mustard and a lot of onions. Ah, this is onion day isn't it?"

"Every day. Something to drink?"

"Water," said Sammy.

"Water," said Brian.

Scott had already ordered and was waiting for his food. "Making any progress on the you-know-what?" he asked softly out of the side of his mouth.

"Even if we solve it, Brian and I aren't sure any objects used to mark the location will still be around. That burial happened two hundred years ago. Any landmarks will probably be gone."

"But it's worth a shot. Agreed?"

Brian didn't like the sound of the word "shot." He didn't want his and Sammy's body to replace the necklace in the ground.

Sammy nodded. "Brian and I will take another look at it this evening."

"I wish I could join you, but I'm driving back to Philly tonight," said Scott. "I just want you to know I'll be back tomorrow."

"Maybe we'll have good news for you then," said Brian.

"Do you know how many miles it is from here to Philadelphia?"

"It's around sixty miles," replied Brian.

"With the heavy traffic, I should be home in one and a half to two hours," said Scott. "I guess I shouldn't complain though. Two hundred years ago it took the stagecoach five days to make the trip."

As the food was being served, Scott asked whether the boys or the police had any information on Karen's whereabouts. But before Sammy answered the question, he received a shock. The customer sitting directly across from them lowered his paper.

He was heavyset and wore a baseball cap, beard, and a mustache.

It was Mr. Arizona himself, Robert Turner!

CHAPTER EIGHT

"**S**ure he was spying on us," said Brian later that evening in Sammy's room. "Heard everything we said, too, I bet. Probably had a super sensitive microphone embedded in his baseball cap. Had a wire running to his hearing aid."

"Oh," said Sammy, "you saw the wire and hearing aid?"

"Well, you couldn't see it. Not with all that fake hair he has on his face."

"It didn't look fake to me," said Sammy seriously.

"It's a disguise. Our Mr. Turner is a thief. Probably wanted by the police all over the United States. Right, Sammy?"

Sammy, seated at his desk, was watching his buddy relaxing on the bed. "The next time you run into Robert Turner, you can pull his beard off. Right now, let's stick to the facts."

Brian muttered something as he raised his notebook. His eyes were now on the notes he held between his face and the ceiling. "You want facts. Here they are. Tom Killian told me he was dating Karen until she disappeared. But Andrea Hill said Karen had stopped seeing him."

"That's interesting," said Sammy. "If he lied about that, what other lies might he tell?"

"His one comment I might believe," said Brian as he flip a page. "Tom said Karen ran away because of her father. Andrea at the restaurant backed that up. She said Karen hated her father because he made her work in the embalming room."

Sammy glanced over at the psychology section in his bookcase. He thought about people's reaction when exposed to death. An individual, who is forced to view a corpse, may experience vivid horrors for life. "You have to be in the right frame of mind to face death," he finally said.

"Yeah, especially your own death," said Brian. "I still dream about my brush with death." He was thinking of the case of the *Bird in the Hand* in which he was held hostage with a ball-point pen pushed against his neck.

"I can't believe Mr. Barton is holding his daughter a prisoner in the embalming room," said Sammy. "But it's possible her father might be responsible for her absence."

"Here's another fact for you," said Brian, finally allowing his arms and notebook to collapse beside him on the bed. "Tom has a temper and is plenty jealous of Scott Boyer. That would give him a reason to write nasty notes about Scott."

Sammy thought a moment. "But the first note mentioned the necklace. How could Tom know about the necklace?"

"It seems to me," said Brian, "everybody knows. You've heard of a gold rush? Get ready for a necklace rush. Yep, right here in our little village of Bird-in-Hand. Soon people will be digging holes all over the place."

"Which means we must hurry and solve this puzzle." Sammy reached into the drawer and carefully placed the journal page copy before him. "Brian, let me throw an idea out to you."

"They're clever," said Brian, indicating he was in a world of his own and had not heard his friend.

"Who's clever?"

"Spiders." Brian raised himself up on one elbow and pointed. "Do you see that spider web over in the corner?"

Sammy turned in his chair. "Yeah, what about it?"

"It's empty," replied Brian. "Larry is hiding. He's smart enough to realize if a fly saw him in the web, he would stay away. So Larry keeps himself hidden. Smart, huh?"

"Your spider friend, Larry, doesn't seem too bright to me," said Sammy. "If he was smart he would know there are no flies in this room. That's why his web is empty."

Not to be outdone, Brian said, "And why are there no flies in this room? Because Larry caught them all. See, that shows how clever he is."

"Brian, I can see now that you are as smart as that spider," said Sammy, returning his attention to the writing.

Brian looked at Sammy and then back at the empty web. He snapped back on the bed and frowned at the ceiling. He knew he had been outdone by his partner.

For the next two minutes, the room was still. Sammy was concentrating on the coded message, while Brian was visualizing his best friend being entrapped in a giant spider web.

Brian finally abandoned the bed and stood by the front window. Tourists were still scampering about, tasting what was left of the day. The village had its own unique flavor at night. Most of the shops were closed. Locals were home. The "big spotlight" had gone down behind the horizon. But the performance was not over. The village continued to enchant those who sampled the night.

But something was wrong. As Brian's eyes swept across Main Street and centered on the Village Inn, he saw it. "Hey, Sammy, the light's on in Scott Boyer's window."

"Are you sure it's his room?" Sammy went to the window. "Yeah, that's his room all right."

"He's supposed to be in Philadelphia," added Brian. "Do you think something's wrong?"

Sammy returned to his desk. "Maybe he changed his mind. Come on. Let's put our energy into solving this puzzle." As he said that, the 60 suddenly jumped from the paper to something he had heard earlier that day. He glared at Brian.

Brian was puzzled. "What? What?" He asked.

"You said that it was sixty miles to Philadelphia." Sammy glanced down and ran his finger under the 60 M to P.

"Sixty miles to Philadelphia," repeated Brian excitedly. Slowly the animation drained from his face. "So it's not the directions to the necklace after all. Jonathan was just recording the miles he traveled."

Sammy's finger continued under X 6 to L. "How many miles from here to Lancaster?"

"Seven or eight," answered Brian. "Old Jonathan was off one or two miles if that's what it implies. Hey, the X could mean he wasn't sure so he took a guess. You know, like in Algebra. X is the unknown."

"Or," said Sammy, "X marks the spot." He grabbed a pen and drew a square around the symbols leaving the X on the outside. "What does that resemble?"

"A box full of letters and numbers," said Brian.

"But if it read sixty miles to Philadelphia and six to Lancaster?"

"Oh, I get it, a road sign!" yelled Brian. "And the X means . . . what?"

A slight smile appeared on Sammy's face. "Jonathan buried the necklace next to the sign," he said proudly. He sat back, relaxed, and folded his arms across his chest. He glanced past Brian to the window. His mind's eye traveled up and down Main Street. The smile faded as a sense of reality overtook the moment. "The bad news is, the road sign is no longer out there."

Brian thought for a moment. "We don't need the sign. All we have to do is find the spot that is sixty miles from Philadelphia and six miles to Lancaster. Right, Sammy?"

"Do you know how accurate road signs are?" asked Sammy. "They can be off by as much as a mile. Also, the city limits of both Philadelphia and Lancaster have changed over two hundred years."

Brian again glanced across the street to the Village Inn. "Scott's light is still on in his room. Let's go over and tell him we solved the puzzle and see what he says."

"No, let's not tell him yet." Sammy paused and then with hope in his voice, said, "Brian, there's still a chance we might be able to get to the necklace."

The large grin on Brian's face reflected what he had always known about his best friend. When faced with what appeared to be a dead-end, Sammy could come up with an answer. "We're going to get a metal detector. Right, Sammy," he said, trying to outguess his partner.

"No, but that might be a good idea," said Sammy, giving Brian credit for the thought.

"What's a better idea than that? Get a necklace sniffing dog?"

"No. Tomorrow morning we're going to pay a visit to the Lancaster County Historical Society."

CHAPTER NINE

This was not the first time the two teenage detectives had ventured into the Lancaster County Historical Society. An English paper for Mrs. Bailey's class last year had required some delving into local history. They signed in at the visitor register and paid the five-dollar fee required of non-members. Sammy entered the fee in his notebook on the page marked expenses.

The card catalog helped the boys to quickly locate books pertaining to both Bird-in-Hand and the Old Philadelphia Pike. They selected two books. The larger book contained information on the history of Lancaster County. And much to their surprise, the other book told the history of just Bird-in-Hand.

"What are we looking for?" whispered Brian as the boys sat at a nearby table.

Sammy handed the larger book to Brian. "Skim for anything about the Old Philadelphia Pike in relation to Bird-in-Hand. Check for any descriptions of road signs. Look for old photographs of scenes taken along the pike. Some of the pictures might show sign posts."

"Gotcha, chief," said Brian playfully and saluted. The serious look he got from his partner sent him quickly to the book's index.

Since the history of Bird-in-Hand started with the construction of the Old Philadelphia Pike, Sammy began skimming the smaller book from page one. Because he was an avid reader, he had trained himself to read groups of words at a time instead of each word individually. This speeded up the reading process immensely.

All the reading Sammy did added to the vast storehouse of knowledge programmed into his brain. Consciously, he couldn't remember everything he read, but he understood the information was recorded somewhere in his brain cells. He was learning grammar, spelling and sentence structure, and storing information that could be used later. Sammy smiled. He enjoyed programming his brain.

Sammy glanced at page two of the book that lay before him. He already knew how the village of Bird-in-Hand had gotten its name. According to legend, in 1734, the Old Philadelphia Pike was being laid out to connect Lancaster to Philadelphia. Two road surveyors were discussing where they would spend the night. Should they stay at the local inn or travel to Lancaster? One surveyor said, "A bird in the hand is worth two in the bush." The other agreed, and so they stayed at what became known as the Bird-in-Hand Inn. Sammy smiled as he looked at the picture of a bird resting in a hand.

Sammy kept reading and turning the pages. Lancaster was known as the *gateway to the west*, he read. Inns were built every few miles along the pike to serve travelers and the animals. The pike was first paved and oiled about 1919. The pike was reconstructed at Bird-in-Hand in 1951.

And then it happened.

He saw the picture—the road sign!

He looked again to make sure.

On page 28, staring boldly at him, was a close-up picture of a stone marker. The rounded top made the marker look more like a tombstone than a road sign. But the markings were exactly as those written in Jonathan's journal. Sammy read the caption under the picture. It stated the stone marker was located between Bird-in-Hand and Smoketown. The marker told travelers they were 60 miles from Philadelphia and 6 miles from Lancaster. The caption also said the information was carved deeply into the stone so that in the dark, persons could feel the letters and numerals and know where they were.

Sammy checked the book's copyright date. 1984. Great! he thought. The stone might still exist. Between Bird-in-Hand and Smoketown. He grabbed the book and stood. "Brian, you can stop. I found it. I found what we need."

Brian didn't move.

Sammy tapped Brian on the head with the edge of the book. "Brian, we hit the jackpot. Put your book back. I found what we were looking for."

"What?" muttered Brian. "You did? What did you find? Oh, okay, let me put the book back first."

"You seem confused, Brian. You didn't fall asleep did you?" asked Sammy.

Brian mumbled something to himself as he shuffled to the bookshelf.

Sammy went to the copy machine and made three copies of page 28. He inspected the copies, was satisfied, and replaced the book on the shelf. After he paid for the copies, he joined Brian who was waiting near the door.

"You only needed to copy one page?" asked Brian, anxious to see what was going to lead them to the necklace.

Sammy handed one copy to Brian and then glanced at his watch. His father had dropped them off and promised to be back in an hour.

When Brian saw the photograph and read the caption, he understood why Sammy had copied only one page. It was true, he thought. A picture *is* worth a thousand words. "Wow! Between Bird-in-Hand and Smoketown," he said. "Will the stone still be there, do you think?"

They devised a plan. Brian was to observe the left side of the road from the back seat of the car. Sammy was in charge of the right side from the passenger seat. Mr. Wilson concentrated on the driving. They didn't want to create a driving hazard for the Amish buggies and the tourists.

The youthful detectives manned their stations as they approached Smoketown from Lancaster. Of course they didn't expect to spot the marker in Smoketown itself, but they were on full alert. They passed the Smoketown Elementary School on the right. This was it. Anytime now. Yes, anytime. Watch. Don't miss it. Scan the area. Soon. Soon.

Then twenty feet ahead of the car.

BIRD-IN-HAND.

The sign said so.

Did they miss the stone marker? Could it still be here along the road? They continued to stare, to hope. The area was hanging on to the past. Couldn't it hang on to the stone marker. Please. Just this once. Please. Just one little stone marker. Be there. Please.

Then it hit them, smashing their expectations. The concrete railroad underpass loomed in front of the car. They were now near the center of the village. All hope was gone.

"It was there, but we missed it. Right, Sammy?" said Brian as the boys stood on the porch of the Bird-in-Hand Country Store. They could easily be mistaken as tourists standing among the Amish quilts and crafts that decorated the porch.

Sammy was downhearted. "I suppose we could have missed it. We definitely will go back. Maybe walk this time for a thorough search. He nodded his head toward the inn. "But first, let's report to Scott

Boyer. He'll be anxious to hear we solved the mystery of the necklace's hiding place."

As if on cue, Scott rounded the corner of the Village Inn. "Sammy, Brian," he yelled, heading for the young detectives and sidestepping the cars and the tourists on the way. "Any luck?"

Sammy's blue eyes wandered up to the back third-floor window of the inn. Strange that Scott should appear so quickly, thought Sammy. He was probably watching from his window. Was he more interested in watching them than being involved in his own research and investigation? Without saying anything, Sammy handed Scott one of the copies showing the stone marker.

"Hey, it's just like in Jonathan's journal." He read the caption. "And the stone marker is—"

"We checked," interrupted Brian. "We didn't find it."

"Sure it's there. Well, it has to be there. Doesn't it?" asked Scott, seemingly confused. "We're close to getting the necklace. I can feel it. Come on, we'll go in my car."

"Did you go to Philly last night?" asked Brian as the trio weaved through the cars and the tourists to the parking lot beside the inn.

"Yes, just got back. I saw you as I was parking my car."

"Your light was on," said Brian.

"What?" asked Scott as if he hadn't heard the teenager.

"The light was on in your room late last night," said Sammy to make the communication clearer.

"Oh, that," said Scott. "I wanted people to think I was still hanging around town."

"Why? If you don't mind my asking," probed Sammy.

Scott's red hair fell over his eyes. "That's my business. It's personal."

As they neared Scott's car, Sammy lost his balance and fell against it. If his upper body hadn't caught the front of the car, he would have landed on the ground. He rubbed his arm and glanced back. Loose stones covered the parking area.

Brian looked at the ground but said nothing. He knew Sammy could be very clumsy at times.

The blue Ford sedan, with three sets of eager eyes aboard, slowly rode the shoulder, allowing other cars and buggies to pass. Their ten-mile-per-hour pace in the forty-miles-per-hour stretch between Bird-in-Hand and Smoketown, made it necessary for them to ride the "buggy lane." The Amish seemed content to share their lane with the "English" man and two boys.

Brian was sure this reversed trip, heading toward Smoketown from Bird-in-Hand, would reverse their luck. It didn't. And as the prospect of finding the stone marker grew weaker, Scott turned right onto Mill Creek Road, pulled to the side, and parked.

An old man was ambling along toward the stove and fireplace shop. He paused and smiled, pleased that some excitement was interrupting his dull day. "Hello."

"Hello. I wonder if you can help us?" asked Scott as he shoved the paper at the old man. "You ever see a stone marker like this?"

The old man moved in close and squinted. "Yep, back in 1938, was the first time I seen it. I moved here that year."

"Where was it when you saw it?" asked Scott.

"Right over there." The old man pointed across the road to his right.

Sammy leaned over from the passenger side. "When was the last time you saw it?" he asked.

"Right now. I'm looking at it." He pointed again.

Sammy and Brian both rushed from the car and followed the wrinkled finger over to the stone slab.

"There, on the grass between the two pine trees. See it?"

They did. The gray swipe of color was perched on a slight embankment in front of a fenced-in field.

The gray stone marker, partly tinted with green mold, blended in with the grass, weeds, and the trees. Facing the road, the rounded-top marker appeared to be a lone tombstone, silently marking a cluster of bones beneath. But for the two would-be sleuths and their client, the stone was a sentinel watching over, not a set of bones, but a set of jewels.

Sammy and Brian thanked the old man while Scott parked the car. Then they hurried across the road to confront history.

The piece of chiseled stone was chipped and weathered. Sammy knelt before the marker and traced his fingers over the worn indented message. It was identical to the copied photograph: 60 M to P 6 to L.

Still numb from the realization that the necklace might lay several feet away, Sammy examined the grassy area to his left. The dirt was hard, solid. His fingers prodded through the grass and weeds. The only break in the surface was a curved crack from dryness. His fingers raked up a few small stones and pieces of dried grass. "Good, nobody has dug here recently," he said.

Brian was beside himself as he glanced at Scott. "Where's a shovel? Let's dig."

Scott looked around then shook his head. "Not now. People will think we're stealing the stone marker. I don't want to draw attention to what we're doing. We'll come back tonight when it's dark."

Because their backs were to the busy road, they didn't observe the black car that slowed traffic as it cruised past them. A full face of hair and a baseball cap filled most of the side window. Quickly the head turned and the black car picked up speed. The mustache and beard separated, revealing a cunning smile.

CHAPTER TEN

The shovel, with a little help from Scott's right foot, broke through the surface. Scott lifted and spilled the clump of sod in front of the boys. Sammy and Brian were prepared to break up the chunks of dirt with their hand tools. Stabbing at the dirt wasn't exactly like panning for gold, but it would enable them to find individual jewels. They had reasoned that two hundred years of being buried, could cause the necklace to break apart.

From across the road, a streetlight's feeble yellow glow added an eerie mood to the setting. The three treasure hunters were nervous but concentrated on the job at hand. Only the moving shadows created by a passing car disturbed the anxious 'grave robbers.'

Brian shook and drops of sweat fell from his face. "I thought you said everyone would be watching the eleven o'clock news."

"Must be a tourist," said Scott, half joking.

"Nothing in this dirt," said Sammy. "Next."

Another shovelful of soil and grass was dumped at the anxious teenagers. Again nothing.

More dirt. Nothing.

"Maybe we're digging at the wrong place," said Brian.

"The X was drawn on the left side," said Scott. "That's where I'm digging." He continued with another shovelful, being careful not to damage the necklace should the shovel strike it. He emptied the heavily ladened shovel onto the mound of dirt already formed in front of the boys.

Something emerged from the chunk of dirt.

Sammy did not need his garden tool this time. The long strip of metal with stones fell away and separated itself from the soil. In Sammy's mind there was no doubt this was the priceless ancient necklace. His fingers caressed the jeweled necklace with reverence. He gingerly raised and shook the artifact, allowing the soil to unwrap itself from the prize. Only then could its size and weight be fully realized.

It appeared to be fifteen inches long and must have weighed two pounds. An intricate design ran through the seven gold pieces hinged together with small golden rings. A large jewel was mounted on each golden panel.

Sammy grasped the free end with his other hand. From his knees he said, "Look," and stretched to raise the necklace higher for the others to see.

"Wow!" said Brian as he stood with his eyes and mouth opened wide. His hand automatically went for the necklace. His finger tips lightly brushed across the protruding curves and edges of the mounted gems.

Scott quickly dropped the shovel, reached over, and pushed downward on Sammy's hands. "Careful. Let's not advertise it. Someone might be watching." He carefully took the necklace from Sammy, turned his back to the road, and in the sparse light inspected the object of his search. "Ain't she a beauty? Jonathan was right. This would be the main attraction at any auction."

Scott glanced around, searching for other eyes that might be prying in the darkness. Feeling safe, he opened a small plastic bag he brought along for the purpose. But as he lowered the dangling necklace into the bag, a low, continuous moan was heard.

"No-o-o-o-o. No-o-o-o-o. St-a-a-ay aw-a-a-ay."

"W-W-What's that?" stammered Brian. "D-Did you hear it?"

They peered beyond the wire fence and into the field. Their faces drained white. Standing before them, in full ceremonial dress, was an Aztec Indian.

Chapter Eleven

The figure wore a long robe and an ornate headdress. The image of the Aztec Indian so surprised the boys that by the time they adjusted to the sight, it was too late. As fast as the ghostly Indian had materialized, it was gone.

"Hey, let's get the dirt back into the hole," yelled Scott, "and get out of here."

No one argued.

The next day turned hectic around noon when Sammy and Brian showed up at the Village Inn at the invitation of Scott Boyer. The boys expected a short chit-chat and thank-you session with their ex-client. Instead, they were instantly bombarded with questions from reporters as they entered the inn. Sammy shook his head. It hadn't taken long for the media to descend on the little village town.

Upstairs in the room with Scott, the questions continued as a local television crew filmed the two local teenage detectives holding the now clean and sparkling Aztec necklace. Scott introduced the boys to a Mr. Domingo Gomez, an expert on Indian artifacts. He had examined the necklace and declared it a genuine Aztec ornament. He certified its gems as a large emerald in the center with three diamonds on each side.

According to Gomez, the gemstones were a peace offering given to the Aztes by an Indian tribe in South America. An Aztec craftsman designed the crescent-shaped gold necklace and attached the gems. It was genuine all right and worth over a million dollars. The video camera panned from Mr. Gomez to a closeup of the necklace.

That evening, the young detectives watched the local television news reports at five and six o'clock. They also read the newspaper account of how Scott Boyer and they had dug up a priceless necklace along the Old Philadelphia Pike. The article also mentioned the apparent curse that accompanied the necklace. One photograph showed them with the ancient artifact. The caption under the picture identified Scott Boyer, Sammy Wilson, and Brian Helm and mentioned their use of an old journal to find the prized necklace. Another photo showed Scott with the appraiser, Mr. Gomez, inspecting the gems.

Brian was standing by Sammy's bedroom window. "See, I told you," said Brian. "We should have charged him for our services. Even the reporters asked if we could get rich from this. We already have enough experience to charge at least a ten percent finder's fee. Let's see. Ten percent of a million is . . . is . . . a lot of money."

"One hundred thousand dollars," said Sammy. "But there's an old saying."

"Yeah, I know it," interrupted Brian. "The rich get richer and the poor get poorer."

"That's not the one I had in mind," said Sammy. "How about, if it sounds too good to be true, it probably is."

"You mean the necklace doesn't exist," said Brian sarcastically.

Sammy, who had been standing, backed up and sat on his desk. "It's not just the necklace. It's this whole caper. This case just doesn't wear right."

"What's that mean? Is that an old Pennsylvania Dutch saying? I never heard that one before."

"Last year my mother bought me new jeans. They were baggy and didn't fit. They just didn't wear right. Well, it's the same with this case. Some parts of it don't fit. This case just doesn't feel right."

"Like what?" asked Brian.

"Like, why did Scott say he went to Philadelphia when he didn't go?"

"How do you know he didn't go?"

"You remember yesterday when I tripped and fell against the hood of Scott's car?"

"Yeah."

"Well, I fell on purpose. The hood of his car was cold."

"So?"

"Scott said he had just gotten back from Philadelphia. The hood of his car should have been at least warm."

"Hey, that was clever," said Brian. "But why would he lie about going there?"

"I've been thinking about that. Doesn't it seem strange for him to ask the distance? He drove here from Philadelphia a week or so ago. It seems he created a reason for us to associate the 60 miles to Philadelphia with the cryptic message."

Brian left the window, sat on the bed, and faced his friend. "You mean he was helping us to solve the puzzle? That doesn't make sense. You're saying Scott already knew what the numbers and letters meant."

"That's the way I have it figured," said Sammy. "But did Scott know Jonathan was describing a road sign? And if he did, did he know where the marker was located?"

Brian relaxed on the bed and purposely gazed at the ceiling. "Why did he want us to discover the meaning of the sign if he already knew it?"

"Let's bat that idea around for a while," suggested Sammy as he walked around the desk and eased himself into his chair.

"Scott wanted to help us with the puzzle without us knowing," said Brian.

"But why? Why was it important for us to be the ones who solved it?"

No answers came.

Sammy shifted in his seat. "And another part of this case that doesn't feel right—"

"You mean that doesn't *wear right*."

Sammy ignored the comment. "If an object is in the ground for two hundred years, it should have been caked with dirt. Last night, when I pulled the necklace from the soil, the dirt particles easily fell away from it. The necklace was dirty, but it was not caked with dirt."

"Are you saying the necklace was put in the ground recently?"

"Something like that."

"But the ground was solid. You said so yourself. Didn't I even see you separate the grass to look?"

"I've been thinking about that." Sammy jumped from his chair. "Follow me. We're going to try a little experiment."

The two boys marched down through the shop to the back porch. Sammy snatched the shovel and went to a dirt strip next to the driveway. "One time I saw my uncle bury an electric cable underground. He did it while barely disturbing the dirt. Watch."

Sammy jumped on the shovel with two feet, driving the blade all the way in. He hopped off and pushed the shovel handle forward, creating a three-inch wide, v-shape opening in the ground. Sammy lifted the shovel out and laid it aside.

"Look," he said and inserted his hand down into the slot. His fingers went down ten to twelve inches. He then withdrew his hand and dropped a stone into the slit in the earth. He stamped his foot and forced the solid dirt back to close the opening. The only mark left on the surface was a curved crack. Sammy pointed. "Last night, I saw a break in the ground just like that one. I thought it was a crack caused by dryness, but . . ." He shrugged and brushed his black hair from his doubting blue eyes.

"So Scott buried the necklace. He then helped us with a clue to its location so we would find it. Sammy, that's nonsense."

"Well, maybe," admitted Sammy. "But what I'm suggesting is the necklace we found is not the one mentioned in Jonathan's journal."

"But how could Scott afford to get his hands on a real Aztec necklace worth over a million dollars?" asked Brian.

A strange look came over Sammy's face. His mental computer was calculating, catching and matching pieces of the puzzle and snapping them together. He grabbed Brian's arm. "Come, Dr. Watson, we must go!"

"Oh, good!" said Brian. "But tell me, Mr. Holmes, is the game afoot?"

"No," answered Sammy. "The game is a book."

CHAPTER TWELVE

The book Sammy had in mind was the visitor register at the Lancaster County Historical Society. The register contained the names of all visitors to the building since January of that year. While Brian kept the attendant busy, Sammy skimmed the names that filled the beginning pages of the book. He was more than pleased with what he found.

Next, he obtained the book on the history of Bird-in-Hand. This was the same book in which he had discovered the picture of the stone marker. He sat at a table and reviewed several pages. The information didn't mean anything at the time he first read it, but now it did. He nudged Brian who was falling asleep next to him. "Brian, wake up. We're going."

Brian's head jerked upwards. "What? I'm not sleeping. I'm just waiting for you."

"As I recall, the last time we were here, your head was down on your book just—"

"Well, I wasn't sleeping. I was reading," interrupted Brian. "I like to get close to the words."

Sammy smiled. "Okay, then tell me one fact you read."

Brian's lips twisted out as he frowned, displaying his thinking mode. After a few seconds his eyebrows lifted. "A lot of trees had to be cut down to build the Old Philadelphia Pike. That information was on page five, second paragraph," he said grinning. "And you thought I was sleeping. Ha! *And . . . sometime in the 1950's, the road was improved. They built shoulders on the road, *for safety reasons*," Brian announced with a flourish.

"Brian, I'm impressed," said Sammy. "Now I know when the buggy lanes were built and why."

Suddenly, as Brian was forming his see-I-told-you-so grin, Sammy jumped up from the table and shook him. "Brian, you're wonderful."

"That's what I keep telling you," kidded Brian. "You're lucky to have such a wonderful guy for a friend."

Sammy pulled on his friend's arm. "Brian, I'm serious. Tomorrow morning we're going to make a special trip to see our friend, Detective Ben Phillips. With what I discovered, plus what you just said, we can prove the necklace we found is not Jonathan's necklace."

CHAPTER THIRTEEN

As soon as the boys entered the police station, they saw the activity and knew that something big was going down.

Detective Phillips exited a room and hurried down the hall toward his office. Seeing his young friends and not missing a stride, he motioned for them to follow him.

"So you've heard the news," said Phillips as he slapped some folders down on his desk.

Sammy and Brian glanced at each other with confusion.

"You haven't heard yet," said Phillips as he noted the blank look on the boys' faces. "I can't believe Bird-in-Hand's famous detective duo haven't a clue as to what's happened."

"What happened?" asked an anxious Sammy.

"The Aztec necklace was stolen six o'clock this morning at the inn."

"Oh, no," said Brian.

"Sammy, how could you have missed the excitement across the street from your shop?"

Sammy thought back to the night before when he decided to sleep over at Brian's house. "I slept at Brian's house last night because it's closer to the station. We wanted to talk to you first thing this morning. But how did it happen? Wasn't the necklace put into a safety deposit box?" asked Sammy.

"Scott Boyer was to take it to the bank this morning. Too late, as it turns out," said Phillips as he grabbed his suit coat from his chair, put it on, and sat facing his file folders.

Even sitting behind his desk, the heavy-set, six-foot-two detective dominated the room. His thin mustache gave him the dapper look. But the morning's intensive investigation had softened his dark and piercing eyes.

"You mean Scott kept the necklace overnight in his room at the inn?" asked Sammy.

"Boy, I wouldn't want to go to sleep with a million-dollar necklace in *my* room," said Brian. "A person could wake up dead."

Detective Phillips took a deep breath and pointed at the two folding chairs that faced his desk. "Have a seat." He opened the top folder and started to read as the young detectives adjusted themselves in their chairs.

"About six o'clock this morning, there was a knock at Scott Boyer's door. He got out of bed, went to the door, and unlocked it. The door was immediately pushed inward, forcing the victim back onto the floor. The intruder, wearing a ski mask, then proceeded to tie his hands and feet with a rope. Once done, he held a knife to the victim's throat and threatened: Quote, 'Tell me where the necklace is, or I'll cut your throat.'"

"So Scott quickly told him, and the necklace and the intruder vanished," added Sammy.

"Well, more or less. Then comes the interesting part," said Phillips. "After the burglar gagged him and left, Scott rolled over to the door, kicked it several times, which got the attention of the innkeeper. After he's untied, he called 911 and reported the incident. And, when we arrived, guess who we found standing behind the inn with a shovel in his hand?"

"Who?" asked Brian, leaning forward in his chair.

Phillips glanced at the report. "Thomas Killian."

"Tom Killian? Karen's boyfriend?" said Sammy.

"Yep, standing there like he's waiting for us," said Phillips.

"And the necklace?" asked Sammy.

"Missing. We searched him and the area. No necklace. We're holding him here as a suspect. In fact I just came from interviewing him when you two arrived."

Sammy was busy trying to fit these new puzzle pieces together. Was Tom Killian somehow connected to the jewels? he wondered. But why remain at the robbery scene? "Why was he there with a shovel?" asked Sammy. "What did he say?"

Detective Phillips stood and headed for the door. "Come on. I'll let you hear it for yourself. He has quite a story to tell. Maybe you can pick up on something I missed."

The Tom Killian seated at the table as the three entered the small room was not the same complacent young man Brian had interviewed at the mall. The tall, thin frame was hunched over with the elbows supporting a worried face. The brown ponytail dangled down the right side of his neck. Tom's mouth forced a smile as he saw familiar faces.

"Thomas, I believe you know Sammy Wilson and Brian Helm," said Phillips. "They'd like to hear your story. Do you mind going over it again?"

"Hi, Brian, Sammy. Hey, what I'm saying is the truth, man. I didn't steal no jewelry." Tom leaned back in the chair, freeing his arms to aid him in telling his story. "Last night the phone rang. The person said if I wanted to find out about Karen, I should be in back of the Village Inn at six o'clock this morning. He said to bring a shovel. Man, that's it. That's all I know."

From the puzzle pieces Sammy had already put together, he half believed what he heard. "Was it a man's voice on the phone?"

"I didn't know who it was, if that's what you mean." Tom's sad eyes looked up as he tried to recall the voice. "It was either a man trying to sound like a woman or a woman trying to sound like a man. I remember that."

Brian watched as Tom's hand flipped his ponytail back over his shoulder. "Did you see anybody when you were waiting behind the inn?"

"No. I already told the cop there," said Tom, pointing to Phillips.

The detective walked around to Tom Killian. "You boys have any other questions you want to ask before I release Thomas?"

Sammy glanced at Brian then back at Phillips. "No. That's it."

The three stood in the hallway and watched as Tom Killian, with shovel in hand, headed for the main door and left the building.

"What do you think? Do you believe him?" asked Phillips, who had been observing Sammy throughout the questioning of Tom Killian.

"What condition were his clothes in when you found him behind the inn?" asked Sammy.

Phillips smiled. "Just as you saw him now. Nothing torn. Nothing out of place. He didn't appear to be someone who had thrown a man to the floor, struggled to tie him hand and foot, and then dug a hole to bury the necklace."

"And the shovel. Was it as clean as I just saw it?" asked Sammy.

"Yep, and no abrasions on his hands," added the detective. "But you already noticed that. Didn't you?"

Sammy shrugged off the compliment. "Yes, and the way this bizarre case is going, I can believe his story."

Phillips pulled the young detectives toward him and watched as a police officer passed them and entered the Communications Room. With no one else in sight, he suddenly said, "I read in the newspapers that you boys actually saw an Aztec Indian ghost the other night. Was it a real ghost?"

"Whoever was chanting said, 'No, stay away,'" answered Sammy. He paused. "Aztec Indians don't speak English."

"Maybe he learned English in ghostland," teased Brian.

Abruptly changing direction, Phillips asked, "Is Scott Boyer paying you for finding the necklace?"

Before Sammy could answer, Brian stood tall and replied, "We don't *usually* charge for our services, but Scott did promise us some money."

"Is there a problem?" asked Sammy as he detected a suspicious tone to Phillips' voice.

"I don't quite buy into Scott Boyer's explanation of the robbery. The average person wouldn't keep a million-dollar necklace in a hotel room with him overnight. Not when it's been advertised in all the papers. And I find it strange that Thomas Killian should get a phone call to be at the inn at the exact time of the theft."

"Sure," said Brian, "Scott faked the robbery. Probably so he didn't have to pay us. And at the same time, he gets Tom Killian arrested so he has Karen Barton all to himself—if she's still alive."

"And I have a theory to add to that," said Sammy. "I believe Scott buried the necklace at the stone marker himself."

The young detectives' statements caught Phillips by surprise. "You're suggesting Scott Boyer buried a million-dollar necklace, had you boys find it, and then staged the robbery to frame Killian?"

"Not a million-dollar necklace," corrected Sammy. "A fake necklace."

Phillips paused as he considered the implication. "But what about the expert? Then you're also saying, the person who examined the necklace and declared it genuine is also a phony," said Phillips as he shook his head. "Sammy, I think you're off the track here. What about the necklace that Jonathan Boyer buried two hundred years ago?"

"I'm starting to think everything about this case is a fake," said Sammy.

"You mean the journal? That Jonathan's journal is a fake? The whole thing is a hoax?" said Phillips. "Scott Boyer did all that to have Karen Barton for himself?"

"I still need another piece to the puzzle to answer that," said Sammy as he dug into his pocket and handed a folded paper to Phillips. "If you could get some background information on that person," he said, pointing to the paper, "we might have the answer to that question."

Detective Marvin Wetzel stuck his head out of the Communication Room. "Ben, we just checked with the pawn shops. The necklace hasn't turned up yet, but they'll keep us posted."

"Okay, thanks," said Phillips. He looked again at Sammy somewhat confused. "Is there any way you can prove the necklace is a fake now that it's reported missing?"

"That may be a problem," said Sammy.

"Hey, we still have pictures of it." said Brian. "The pictures in the newspaper. They are in color, too."

Both Sammy and Phillips glanced skeptically at Brian.

"I know that pictures in the paper are made up of a series of dots, but if we could get the original . . ." Brian shrugged and looked away, feeling he had made another goofy statement hardly worthy of a developing detective.

Sammy's face brightened. His blue eyes sparkled. "Brian, that could be our only hope. What a great idea."

His friend's statement quickly put a smile on Brian's face. "It seemed the only logical answer," bragged Brian, trying to regain his status as a super sleuth. "After all, they say a picture is worth a thousand words."

"All we need is for the picture to say the jewels are not real. That they are imitations," replied Sammy. "Detective Phillips, do you know anyone at the newspaper office who can get us an enlargement of that closeup shot of the necklace?"

"Sure do. In fact, I'll try to get the negative and take it to a one-hour lab. But who's going to make the picture talk?" joked the detective.

"Only one person has eyes more penetrating than yours," said Sammy. "When he looks at a gem, even a photograph, he can make it talk. That man is Ron Finch."

CHAPTER FOURTEEN

The jeweler leaned toward the colored photograph that lay before him. The five-powered head visor he wore hovered over the photo. Brian had picked up the large, detailed photograph from Photo Mart. At the same time, Sammy had arrived at Miller's Jewelry Store and explained his suspicions to Mr. Ron Finch, jeweler and gemologist. Ron's knowledge and skill with gems made him well-known throughout the area.

Suspense was building as Sammy and Brian watched the jeweler examine the details in the enlargement of the seven jewels. Ron's head floated from gem to gem pausing briefly at each one. Finally he lifted his head, slid off the magnifying aid, and announced, "They're all fake."

Yes! Sammy thought to himself. His smile was one of relief. Now he knew he was right in suspecting the necklace to be a phony. The feeling he experienced was the same as when he discovered a solution to any problem: great satisfaction. Now he was eager to learn more. "How can you tell the stones aren't real?"

Ron pointed to a small flake of light in the photograph. "See that white streak in the emerald? That's where the light hit an imperfection in the gem. A bright spot like that indicates an air bubble." He handed the magnifying head visor to Sammy. "Look for yourself."

Sammy gingerly slid the visor over his head and adjusted the lens down over his eyes. He varied the distance between his head and the photo until the image became sharp. And there it was. The light was reflecting from an air bubble in the jewel. "Yes, I see the circle. It kind of looks like a donut." Sammy leaned back and handed the visor magnifier to Brian. "But can't real gems have air bubbles?"

As Brian was taking a look, Ron Finch explained. "If the emerald and diamonds were genuine, the flaws would appear dark in the photo. Also the flaws would have an irregular, elongated shape, not round. Mother Nature does not put air bubbles in natural stones. Only man does that."

"I see it," said Brian. "It does look like a donut."

"Brian, move your head over to the diamond, left of the emerald," said Ron. "Do you see any more white spots?"

Brian's head swung to the left and then hesitated. "Yeah, how about that? Two more donuts."

"Also," said Ron, "do you notice how the emerald seems to be one solid vivid green color?"

Both boys nodded.

"Again Mother Nature does not give us nice even coloring in her crystals. There will always be a range from light to dark coloring in the stones."

Sammy and Brian thanked Ron for his valuable help in confirming the jewels were imitations. Now they had the proof they needed. The excitement showed on their faces as they hurried from the jewelry store and mounted their bikes. The cardboard cylinder, with the photo rolled safely inside, went with them, back to the police station and Detective Ben Phillips.

The teenagers squeezed into their chairs and watched as Detective Phillips held a small magnifying glass over the curled print. They had explained everything the jeweler had said. Now they waited for his reaction to the evidence that lay before him.

Finally he laid the glass aside, looked up, and folded his large hands over the print. "Yes, everything you told me is here." He puckered his lips and shrugged. "But what does it mean? Only that this necklace, Scott Boyer claimed was real, is a phony. And so is Domingo Gomez who appraised it. But no crime has been committed. At most, it's a hoax with no one hurt."

Sammy was heartbroken. His sad blue eyes showed his disappointment.

"The only one hurt," said Brian, "would be the person who stole the necklace from Scott, *if it was stolen*. The thief has a necklace he thought was worth a million dollars. And now he can't sell it. Who would buy a fake?"

Sammy thought about that. Somewhere in all of this scam there had to be a punch line. With all the money being spent to develop this complex deception, there had to be a payoff. But what was it? He glanced at Phillips, and a thought occurred to him. "Did you have time to get a rundown on the name I gave you?"

Phillips reached for a printout resting under his folders and scanned it quickly. "Yeah, I grabbed it from the computer and skimmed it before you came in." He handed the sheet to Sammy. "The sheet also contains Scott Boyer's history of minor arrests."

In their cramped quarters, Sammy didn't have to lean much to share the information with Brian.

As Sammy read the report, a new theory started to form. He glanced at Scott's record printed at the bottom. What he read didn't surprise him. He returned the printout and watched as the detective reviewed it again.

Phillips' mustache twitched as he studied the information. Then without warning his deep penetrating eyes settled on Sammy. "If we can show a connection between this guy and Scott, we might prove criminal intent."

"And if we can prove the necklace wasn't stolen?" said Sammy.

"Filing a false report is a misdemeanor," replied Phillips. "The worst that could happen to Scott would be probation."

A stillness settled over the small, stuffy room as Sammy propped his right hand under his chin and closed his eyes.

Brian watched Sammy, knowing his brain was logically thinking through the problem and producing a plan.

It did.

"All we have to do is get Scott to call the person who's running the operation," said Sammy. Is it possible to put a tap on Scott's phone at the inn?"

Phillips shook his head. "No. We have no criminal evidence. And it is illegal to tape-record someone without their consent."

"So how can we put a stop to their elaborate hoax?" Sammy asked of himself.

"Oh, I know!" shouted Brian. "I could hide in his room and listen in on any conversations."

"And where would you hide in the room?" asked Sammy. "You were there. The room is too small."

"How about the closet?"

"There is no closet in the room," said Sammy. "The old inns weren't built with closets."

Brian wouldn't give up. "Okay, I'll stand outside his door and listen at the keyhole."

Sammy smiled and nodded. Since they couldn't legally put a tap on the phone line, he saw his partner's idea as the next best way to go. "Well, Brian, it's worth a try."

Brian sat tall and looked at Phillips. "It's not illegal to listen, is it?"

The tall detective grinned as he stood and headed for the door. "No, it's not." Suddenly he turned back. "Sammy, I'm curious. How are you going to get Scott to phone his accomplice?"

"I'm going to pull a little scam of my own."

CHAPTER FIFTEEN

According to Richmond Young, Scott Boyer had not been in his room at the inn all day. And from what Sammy had inferred from the evidence so far, it was logical to think that Scott was out looking for Karen and not the necklace.

The light in Scott's room went on about eight o'clock that evening. Sammy stood back from his bedroom window that overlooked Main Street. He waited as he continued to observe the lighted window on the third floor of the inn. He wanted to give Brian ten minutes to cross the street, enter the inn, and establish himself outside Scott's door.

And now it was time.

The young detective took a deep breath and picked up the phone next to his computer. His hands were sweaty as he dialed the memorized number.

"Hello," said an anxious voice immediately after the first ring.

"Hi, Scott. This is Sammy Wilson."

"So you heard about the necklace being stolen."

"Yes, I heard, but I don't believe it."

"Yeah, well, it was stolen this morning," said Scott, not fully understanding what Sammy's words implied.

Sammy figured it was time to jump in and get wet. "I wonder if the thief knew the jewels were imitations?"

"Imitations? I don't understand."

"Come on now, Scott. You and I both know the necklace was not stolen, and that it is a fake just like you." Sammy's heart was beating faster.

"You shut up! You don't know what you're talking about! The robbery was real and the jewels are real."

"The only thing real in this case is that Karen Barton is missing. Do you know anything about that?" asked Sammy, suspecting the answer.

Pause.

"I . . . You may think you're a great detective, but you can't prove anything."

"Sorry, Scott, but I can prove *you* buried the necklace next to the marker. And I can prove the seven stones in the necklace are glass. Just glass."

"Yeah, well, how are you going to prove the Aztec necklace isn't real? Remember it's missing."

"Was that the reason for the fake robbery? So the necklace wouldn't be available for an honest appraisal? Or maybe to frame Tom Killian?"

"I don't know what you're trying to do here, Sammy, but stay out of my face, or I'll come over and break your arms!" shouted the hot-headed redhead, revealing his true nature.

"I'll tell you how I can prove it, Scott. You remember that nice colored closeup shot taken of the necklace by the newspaper photographer?"

Pause.

"Yeah, so what?"

"Air bubbles."

"Air bubbles? What are you talking about?"

"A good friend of mine, a local jeweler, examined the enlargement containing all seven jewels. And he found air bubbles in each one of them."

"Yeah?" said Scott.

"Yeah," repeated Sammy. "Real gems don't have air bubbles. I guess the fake 'expert' you brought in to declare the gems real, needed glasses."

An awkward pause developed, and Sammy could almost feel the heat from Scott's silent rage.

"And Scott, here's where you really messed up. In order to put your scheme into operation, you had to do some research on the history of Bird-in-Hand and the Old Philadelphia Pike. But you didn't do your homework well. You missed something."

"And what was that?" said Scott.

"You missed the one fact that proves you planted the necklace next to the road marker. The fact is that the pike in the Bird-in-Hand area was rebuilt in 1951. Shoulders were added to make the road wider."

Another pause.

"So, what does that prove?" asked the redhead, sounding greatly frustrated.

"It means with the enlarging of the road to double its width, the stone marker was moved." announced the young detective. "And if the marker was moved to its present location in 1951, Jonathan's necklace wouldn't have moved with it."

Another long pause.

The silence told Sammy the time had arrived for some bluffing. "Scott, if you can prove that the journal and the necklace are real, meet me here at the shop tomorrow evening at nine o'clock. That gives you one day. After that, I'll make sure every newspaper and every television station hears about your hoax."

"Sammy, you're out of your mind." There was a pause. "Even if they are fakes, so what? We—I didn't break any laws. It was just a joke on you and Brian. Nobody's hurt. I don't have to prove anything."

Now was the time for Sammy to bet it all. "Maybe I know what your *real* scam is."

A pause.

Sammy continued. "Maybe it's a scheme to make somebody a millionaire."

"You're way off base here, Sammy." Scott paused. "Okay, tomorrow evening at nine. I'll bring the proof."

"Good," said Sammy. "The shop will be closed, and my parents will be upstairs. Just knock at the front door."

"Yeah, okay."

Sammy's hand was shaking as he maneuvered the receiver back into its cradle. It was rough acting tough.

Brian was almost there. He mounted the steps leading to the third floor. I have to be careful, he thought to himself, after swallowing deeply. He glanced behind him. I have been sent on this dangerous mission, but I can handle it. Yep, I just have to act natural. I'll walk up these stairs like a normal person. And because I am a great detective and a fantastic actor, I can pull this off, he thought to himself.

Without warning, a muffled voice came from behind the jittery boy detective. "How can you do this?"

Brian stumbled on a step. "What? Who?" He caught himself on the banister and swung around. He flailed his arms as if to ward off monsters from outer space. His breathing deepened. He twisted his head to locate the direction of the voice.

He saw no one.

"You give me no other choice," continued another muddled voice through a wall of a room on the second floor.

"It's television," said Brian to himself as beads of sweat formed on this forehead. His heart was pounding. He sat on a step and rested.

Minutes passed. He stood, turned, and took another step. The stairway creaked, expressing the fate of old age. Five more steps to go. What if someone came out of one of the rooms? he wondered. His legs were shaking, rattling, and rolling without the aid of music.

"Just be cool," he said under his breath. "Pretend you are a guest in the inn. In the inn," he repeated to himself. "I'm in the inn. I'm in the inn," he sang, putting a tune to the words. "I think I have the makings of a song there."

His feet somehow landed him on the third floor. He snuck to the Bousman Room and leaned against the wall, to the right of the door. He leaned toward the door and listened. He could hear Scott talking to Sammy on the phone. He wiped the droplets of water from his eyes and glanced up and down the hallway.

It was clear. At least for now.

Brian was ready. That afternoon he had put together an electronic listening device. The miniature amplifier rested in his right jean pocket. A hole at the bottom of the pocket allowed a pencil-thin mike to travel down his right leg and exit at shoe level.

Brian knelt on one quivering knee. He pulled out the mike that was tucked into his right sneaker and unwrapped some cord from around his ankle. His trembling fingers pinched the thin black cable and slowly fed the mike under the door. He listened for a reaction from within the room. None came.

Good so far.

Brian's body was shaking as he stood, reached into his pocket, and pushed a button. He heard the faint click. Next he inserted a small earphone into his ear. The long thin cord ran down to the amplifier in his pocket. He prayed the electronic intrusion into the room would not be noticed as Sammy kept Scott busy with his plan.

Five minutes later when Scott made a hurried phone call, Brian and his electronic ear were ready.

"Hi, Mr. Turner, it's Scott Boyer . . . I know I wasn't to contact you anymore, but we have trouble," came the voice loud and clear through the earphone. "Our boy detectives found out about the fake stones in the necklace . . . Air bubbles . . . Yeah, air bubbles. They had a jeweler look at a blowup of a photograph of the necklace. He saw the air bubbles . . . Hey, I didn't make the mistake. You did. You were there. You could have . . . Well, it's too late now. If we can't prove the journal and necklace are real, he's going to tell the news media . . . It surprised me, too . . . Tomorrow night at nine, over in the store . . . It's closed then. His parents will be upstairs in their apartment . . . The parents? I don't know . . . Just Sammy and Brian I suppose . . . Hey, *I'm* not going to rough them up. Anyway, I don't think you can scare them. They're smart, and they're popular here in the village . . . They're going to tell the media about your little charade unless we make them change their minds . . . I know we haven't broken any laws—except a false robbery claim . . . Sure if the police find out, I'll get probation. But it's on *my* record . . . It will be better if you . . . I realize you already paid me for my work, but

I'm out of it now . . . Okay, it's worth a try if you think they'll scare . . . Well, I won't do it. I can't afford any more trouble. I've stopped drinking . . . I got me a girl here . . . Yeah, the girl that disappeared . . . Well, do what you want . . . Sure send somebody . . . Okay, what's his name . . . Wait till I write it down . . . Chuck McCoy . . . The Lancaster Airport. From Chicago. Should I pick him up? . . . But will he know to come to the Village Inn? . . . Yeah, I'm in the Bousman room . . . Hey, it's your show. I could care less . . . Yeah, good-bye."

By ten o'clock that same evening, Sammy, Brian, and Detective Ben Phillips were gathered in Sammy's bedroom. Sammy sat at the desk. Phillips sat motionless on the rocker. Brian took his horizontal position on the bed. His eyes stared blankly at the ceiling. Brian reported what he could recall from the conversation between Scott and Robert Turner.

Sammy was in deep thought as Brian finished. His somber face showed no emotion or even a hint of his thought processes. Sammy waited for any further reactions from his partner. Finally he peered at Phillips. "There it is. Scott *is* working with Turner. Now we can put a stop to Turner's scam."

The rocking chair moved but went nowhere. "It's the other part of the conversation that scares me," said Phillips. "Your 'Let's-shake-them-up' ploy unleashed a demon. Sounds like a probe is going to be sent this way to test your backbone. And the probe's name is Chuck McCoy."

Without warning Brian flipped up from the bed and stood. "We're in deep water this time. Right, Sammy?" He walked to the door. "I have to go to the bathroom."

Sammy cleared his throat. "From what Brian said, Scott has been paid off for his part in the hoax. I thought Scott was still hanging around town pretending to be involved with the recovery of the necklace. But it must be because of Karen. And if that's true, Karen is headed for a lot of trouble. According to the report we read on Scott, he's a hotheaded thug."

"If we're right about the robbery report being false," said the detective, "then Turner has the fake necklace in his possession back in Arizona. And Scott remains here, looking for his lost love." Phillips raised his hands and shook his head. "Hey, we have half the police department investigating Karen's disappearance. I don't know how Scott expects to find her."

"I keep wondering if things would have been different if Karen and Scott hadn't met," said Sammy.

The detective shrugged. "Who knows? I can't understand why Karen would want to date a creep like Scott in the first place."

"He fooled Brian and me, too, remember? We fell right into their plot," said Sammy as he walked around his desk to the window overlooking Main Street. "If we had known from the beginning—"

Sammy stopped. His head turned to his left. His eyes zoomed in on Karen's aunt and uncle's store. Suddenly something clicked. More pieces of the puzzle came together.

"Well, don't worry about Chuck McCoy," said Phillips, interrupting Sammy's thoughts. "We have the advantage of knowing he'll be here tomorrow. I can take care of him."

Sammy's new segment of the puzzle was pushed aside for the moment. He smiled for the first time that evening and faced Phillips. "Thanks. It's great to have a police detective *and* a bodyguard as a friend." He paused and the smile wilted on his face. "But Scott is still the problem."

Brian returned and flopped on the bed, sitting with his feet dangling over the edge. "What did I miss? Did you make all our problems go away while I was gone?"

"Go away," muttered Sammy as he stepped over to his desk. "Not a bad idea, Brian. Yes, there has to be a way that we can—" With a sweep of his hand, Sammy cleared the middle of the desk and sat. He had some thinking to do.

Brian was still and stared at his friend's face. He had seen that expression before. Sammy was planning something big! But what more was there to this case? he wondered. What did Sammy and the detective talk about when he was gone from the room? And something else he didn't understand. Robert Turner had the fake necklace. So what? He hadn't broken any laws. Brian scratched his head and quietly laid back on the bed. He searched the ceiling for his spider friend, but the ceiling was empty. Just like this case, he thought, a big bunch of nothing.

It startled everyone when Sammy suddenly slid off the desk. Raising his arm, he glanced at his watch. He looked at Phillips. "Do you have time tonight to test out one of my theories?" he asked.

The detective took a peek at his own watch. "My wife is home waiting for me, but if I tell her, 'I'm out with the boys,' she won't mind. She likes you guys. She says you make my job easier for me."

"It could happen again tonight if my calculations are correct," answered Sammy as he again looked at his watch. "Brian, we promised your mother you'd be home by ten. You better go. But do me a favor. When you get home, call John Smucker. Ask him if he and Detective Ben Phillips can make a surprise inspection of the restaurant in about thirty minutes. If he can, tell him the detective will meet him at the restaurant. Then give us a call here then and let us know what he says."

Brian bounced from the bed, smiled, and in his best secret agent voice, said, "Right, chief." He paused at the door. "Aren't you and I going along on this caper?"

Sammy shook his head. "Not tonight."

The smile disappeared from Brian's face and he was gone.

Sammy spent the next twenty minutes explaining to Phillips what he should look for at the restaurant and about his plan for tomorrow. Phillips could only shake his head and marvel at the way the fifteen-year-old boy could plot such an elaborate plan. Along the way, Sammy agreed to some minor changes suggested by the detective. They were interrupted only by Brian's phone call to "report in" that John Smucker was available to meet "you know who" at "you know where."

As Detective Ben Phillips departed for the restaurant, he looked back at the confident young detective. "Be careful tomorrow, Sammy. Remember, the good guys don't always win."

CHAPTER SIXTEEN

The country store on Main Street had closed for the night. Two amateur sleuths took their position opposite the door with their backs to the old Coca Cola cooler. Benches with Amish dolls, birdhouses, and signs that fronted the counters created a narrow aisle to the closed entrance. The scent of spices, doubt, and fear filled the hot, stuffy air.

"I hope you know what you're doing," said Brian, who had just returned from a one-day trip with his parents. Minutes before, his partner had hurriedly filled him in on what was to happen when Scott Boyer arrived. But that didn't help him fully understand what was really going on. What if Scott showed up with a gun? Then what? What if Scott didn't show up at all? What if . . .

The shop was now quiet. The "closed" sign on the door faced the street. It was almost nine o'clock. Sammy's parents were waiting upstairs along with

Detective Phillips and a very nervous and frightened young girl. Several undercover policemen were stationed at various areas outside the shop.

And then it happened—too soon. Two figures appeared at the door. It's abrupt opening caused the door to slam back against the merchandise-filled wall, sending several pieces to the floor. The "closed" sign flipped out and reverse itself. Ready or not, the shop was now "open for business."

Only the night lights were on in the shop. The unexpected loud intrusion plus the yellowish illumination from the streetlight gave the two intruders a menacing appearance.

Sammy and Brian backed up until they were almost against the Coca Cola cooler. "Hi, Scott. I see you brought a friend," said Sammy.

"Yeah, the license plates on cars keep telling me, I've got a friend in Pennsylvania. Well, this is him. His name is Chuck McCoy. Chuck, this is Sammy and Brian."

The middle-aged, muscle-bound thug frowned and groaned at the boys. He was taller and much wider than Scott.

"Hi, C-C-Chuck," stammered Brian, moving closer to his partner.

Sammy nodded.

Scott grabbed the edge of the door and slammed it shut. "I hope you don't mind if I take a look around while you look my friend over."

The teenage detectives remained quiet.

Scott Boyer quickly inspected the four small rooms that made up the first floor of the building. He glanced up the flight of steps that led to the apartment. He could hear the television laughing through a closed door.

"We're alone," said Sammy. "My parents are upstairs. Did you bring your proof?"

Without warning, Chuck McCoy moved toward the boys. "You're messing with my friend here, and I don't like that. He has a bad temper, but I don't. Guess what I have?" His right hand snapped up, holding the largest gun Sammy had ever seen. Boys, this is a G-U-N. Guess what that spells?"

"G-G-Gun," said Brian before he realized that Chuck wasn't conducting a spelling lesson.

Scott Boyer reacted as horrified as did the intended victims at the unexpected appearance of the large weapon.

"No, it spells death," continued McCoy. "And Scott here wants me to teach you boys a lesson."

The noise of the exploding gun was deafening. The old wooden building trembled in reaction to the gun's exploding gases. Brian stood in disbelief, stunned by the unexpected gun shot. Sammy's body recoiled back, his hands automatically clutching at his chest. The blood spilled through his fingers and ran down his shirt. He collapsed on the bare wooden floor.

"Sammy! Sammy!" cried Brian. Tears filled his eyes as he dropped beside his friend. "Don't die! Don't die!"

Scott gripped Chuck McCoy's arm holding the gun. "No! No! you dumb idiot!" he shouted at McCoy. "You were supposed to scare him, not kill him!" He backed to the door. "I . . . I want no part of this!" He grabbed for the door, rushed out, and bolted across the street to the inn.

Detective Phillips barreled down the steps. He saw McCoy with the gun. Brian was slumped over his best friend, hugging and shaking him. "Brian," said Phillips.

Brian looked up and yelled, "He's still alive! I know he is! Call 911! Call 911! Hurry!"

The detective stood there without moving. Then he smiled. "Brian, he's all right. Sammy's all right."

"But," said Brian as he looked again at the motionless body he was holding.

Sammy's eyes sprung open. "Hi, Brian. Don't squeeze me too much, I might really die."

"You mean . . . Then you're not . . . This was all . . ." Brian released his grip on his buddy and stood. He didn't know whether to laugh or cry. He peered at the man behind the gun. He, too, was grinning now.

Phillips patted the man's shoulder. "Brian, meet Jimmy Ford, a cousin of mine. He helps me out occasionally on special assignments. I met the 'real' McCoy at the airport and convinced him to return to Chicago on the next plane."

"How did you do that?" asked Brian, wiping the tears from his eyes.

"It's amazing what a badge and a few convincing words can do," said the detective.

"Plus a certain look from those eyes of yours," added Sammy from the floor.

"Not really. I just held up a blank cassette tape and mentioned that it contained a telephone conversation explaining the reason for his arrival. I convinced him to return to Chicago, keep quiet, and collect his money for doing the job. He left with a smile on his face when I told him I would do the job, and Robert Turner would never know the difference."

Jimmy Ford nodded and handed the gun containing blanks to Phillips. Then, turning to Brian and using the same rough voice he had used before, teased, "Are you positive that G-U-N spells gun?"

Brian looked down at Sammy who was still on his back, grinning. "I can't be sure of anything. And you!" He placed his foot on his friend's stomach. "I'm never letting you get up. You can stay on this floor forever, or until you really die—whichever comes first."

"Hey, you're not mad at me, are you, Brian?"

Brian pressed down hard with his foot. "You wouldn't let me in on your plan, would you?"

"I wanted you to react naturally to my death. Otherwise, Scott might not have bought it."

"Are you saying my acting isn't good enough?" Brian said sharply, applying more pressure with his foot.

Sammy grabbed his friend's leg and pushed up. "You do tend to get a little melodramatic sometimes."

Brian crunched up his face. "Hey, is this really fake blood I"m stepping in?"

"It better be," said Sammy as he pushed Brian's foot aside and stood.
"It's the fake blood from my Halloween make-up kit."

The sudden opening of the door drew everybody's attention to the undercover police officer who stood there. "Ben, he's gone. Scott hightailed it up to his room, came out with a suitcase, and whipped out in his car, heading west. Seems he couldn't leave town fast enough."

Sammy smiled with satisfaction.

"Just what we were counting on," said Phillips. "Thanks, Ron. Tell the others it's over. They can go." He shook hands with his cousin. "Thanks Jimmy. You did a terrific job. Tell your wife I'm sorry I kept you out so late."

When the door closed, the detective moved to the stairway. "Scott Boyer is gone. You can come down now!" he yelled.

Sammy's anxious parents hurried down the steps followed by a hesitant, frail-looking young girl. Her frightened blue eyes darted around the shop. Her body quivered as she forced herself to confront the room in which her greatest enemy had stood just minutes before.

"It's okay, Karen. He really is gone," said Sammy. "Scott is gone for good."

Brian was trying to understand Karen's part in all of this. Why did she put that sign on the door? Why hide in the restaurant? Why was she so afraid of Scott Boyer? And he was eager to know why Karen had gone to such drastic measures to escape from Scott. After all, she must have liked him, she dated the guy. Finally he blurted out, "Karen, why are you so terrified of Scott?"

"Brian, not now," said Sammy as he glanced at Phillips as though to apologize.

"No, it's okay. I have her statement back at the station," said Phillips. "Got it last night after John Smucker and I found her hidden away in a large storage closet at the restaurant. It will do her good to talk about it, if she wants." The detective pulled a bench over for Karen to sit and relax.

"Do you want to talk about it, Karen?" asked Sammy's mother.

Karen nodded, and as soon as she sat on the bench, it all poured out. She couldn't stop it. "Scott had been drinking when he pick me up for our date. And before the evening was over, he told me things he wasn't to tell anyone. About how he was from Arizona and was doing a special undercover job. Said his boss was a consultant who advised rich investors. He bragged about how he buried a necklace in the ground and was going to get Sammy Wilson and Brian Helm to find it. And when I asked him why?" Karen lowered her head, "he pull out a knife and held it at my face."

"Why that—" said Brian as the others shook their heads in disbelief.

"Said it was none of my business to know why," she continued. "He said he had talked too much. And now it was our secret. He said if I told anyone about it, he would kill my aunt and uncle. He said when his work was done here, he might take me with him back to Arizona, if I wanted to go."

"The guy's nuts," said Brian.

"Did you ever think of going to the police?" asked Sammy.

"Sure I thought of it. Then I remembered the television shows where police couldn't help until you are attacked or killed or something. I couldn't prove anything. So I—"

Sammy jumped in. "So you told your story to your best friend, Andrea Hill. She somehow arranged for you to hide in the restaurant. Next you posted the sign 'will return in five minutes' and then snuck over to the restaurant."

"Andrea and I had this plan. I would disappear for awhile, until Scott was gone. It was Andrea's idea to make my disappearance mysterious. You know, to make Scott think something really did happen to me. She fixed up some blankets for me in the far end of the storage closet in the lower level of the restaurant." A hint of a smile broke through her nervousness. "I love to read, so Andrea supplied me with a flashlight and lots of books."

"You stayed there during the day," continued Sammy. "After the restaurant closed, you became the 'ghost' that wandered around, stretching your legs and looking for something to eat."

"At first, I was careless. I ate and dropped crumbs. I left doors open. When I bathed in the restroom and stood in the hall to dry my hair, the water dripped on the floor and left a puddle. Then Andrea warned me to be more careful."

Sammy nodded his head. "And it was you who wrote the notes, warning us about Scott."

"Yeah, I had to tell someone. Andrea mailed my first letter and later put my note on Brian's bicycle." Karen looked at Detective Phillips. "You're positive he won't come back?"

"He won't be back. Not now that he thinks he's facing a murder charge." Phillips faced Karen. "This is why I wanted you here. So you could see for yourself what a coward Scott was. He ran at the first sight of trouble. *He won't be back*," repeated Phillips to reassure Karen that she was safe.

Karen stood, more confident of herself. "If it's okay, I'd like to go over to see my aunt and uncle. And I want to call my parents."

"I'll escort you over," said Phillips. "And maybe I can help explain to them why you did what you did."

Karen turned to the Wilsons. "And thank you for hiding me here last night and today. You're kind people."

Phillips held the door. "Come on, Karen. Let's get you back to your family."

"Yes, I have some explaining to do. Don't I?"

"This has been a real experience for all of us," said Sammy, standing there with fake blood still splattered over his clothing and hands.

"How can you call it real?" asked Brian, "Everything about this case was a fake. Jonathan's journal was a fake. The necklace was a fake." He pointed to Karen. "Your disappearance was faked." His hands flew up as he faced his partner. "Sammy, Chuck McCoy was a fake. And let's not forget your fake death, using fake blood."

Sammy went behind the counter, tore off some paper towels from a roll, and wiped some of the sticky stain from his hands. "Brian, you missed another fake—Domingo Gomez, the artifact appraiser." He picked up the newspaper from the counter and pointed to the picture they recognized as Domingo Gomez. Then taking a black pen, Sammy drew a beard and mustache on the face. Finally, he added what was to be a baseball cap.

"Hey, that's Robert Turner," said Brian. "He shaved off his beard and mustache, took off the baseball cap, put on a suit, and became Gomez."

"Right," said Sammy. "He's probably in Arizona right now letting the hair grow back so he can become Robert Turner again."

Brian was feeling better after the shock of his friend's "death" and "resurrection." He stood tall, pulled up his jeans, and grinned. "You knew Turner was running the show when you found his name in the historical society's sign-in book. Right, Sammy?"

"Back in February, Turner was researching the information he needed to produce the fake journal," said Sammy. "Then he had the phony necklace made. He hired Scott to slip into town, bury the necklace, then establish himself in the Village Inn. Robert Turner also registered at the inn as a tourist to keep an eye on his developing con game."

"When I ran a check on Turner's background," added Phillips, "we discovered he was a seasoned confidence man. Currently, in Arizona, he was acting as a consultant to investors."

"But what was this whole scam or hoax about?" asked Brian, hating to admit his lack of understanding. "What was so important about having us dig up a worthless necklace?"

"That was the genius of his plan," said the teenage detective. "To Turner and the world, the necklace wasn't worthless." Sammy pointed to the newspaper headlines. "It was a necklace recovered by two small-town, respectable teenagers. It was appraised by an 'expert' as worth over one million dollars. All the newspapers and television said so. The new-found necklace didn't have to be real as long as nobody suspected it to be fake. He even threw in that the necklace was cursed and produced an Indian ghost to prove it."

Phillips chimed in. "All Turner has to do is walk in and flip the newspaper articles in front of an unscrupulous private collector. He gives the collector time to read the articles, then gently dangles the "stolen" jeweled necklace in front of the collector. The collector holds and feasts his eyes on the necklace that everyone is talking about. He has to have it. He wants to possess what others can't have. This gives him a feeling of power."

Sammy folded his arms over his chest and leaned back against the counter. "A wealthy art collector, who has more money than brains, will pay Mr. Turner nearly a million dollars. He'll then take the necklace and add it to his other treasures in a hidden vault somewhere."

"Brian, you would be surprised," said Phillips, "at the number of imitations that can be part of a collector's treasures. And he's not even aware of it."

"Are you saying Mr. Turner is going to get away with his scam?" asked Brian.

"No, he's not," said Phillips, "because you boys upset his plans. The one thing that Turner counted on to promote his scheme turned against him. He didn't realize just how good you boys are."

Brian's chest puffed out. He glanced at Sammy, winked, and nodded his head. Sammy took the compliment in stride and shrugged, allowing his hands to end up in his pockets.

"Tomorrow morning I will hold a press conference," said Phillips. "By tomorrow evening the whole world will know the necklace and Robert Turner are fakes. As the cowboys used to say, 'We cut them off at the pass.' Hey, we have to go. See you boys tomorrow." He followed Karen out and gently closed the door behind him.

"I hope everything works out for Karen," said Mrs. Wilson. Shaking her head, she added, "It's people like Robert Turner and Scott Boyer who take the fun out of life."

"Well, you know what I always say," said Brian.

Mr. Wilson spoke up. "Something like, 'It's the harsh winters that make you appreciate spring?'"

"No. I always say, 'If you chew gum, life's going to be sticky,'" said Brian, displaying a large grin.

Everybody laughed.

Mr. Wilson took his wife by the arm. "Come on, Helen, let's go to our safe little world upstairs."

As the Wilsons disappeared up the stairway, Brian gazed at his friend. "I have to go, too." He paused. "You know, Sammy, something else was a fake, too."

"Yeah? What's that?"

"Your acting," said Brian.

"You mean—"

Brian opened the front door and reversed the sign to read "closed." He nodded, placed his hands to his chest, and moaned, "Yeah, I could have died better." He dramatically slouched across the porch and faded into the night.

———

SAMMY AND BRIAN MYSTERY SERIES

#1   **The Quilted Message** by Ken Munro
The whole village was talking about it. Did the Amish quilt contain more than just twenty mysterious cloth pictures? The pressure was on for Bird-in-Hand's two teenage detectives, Sammy and Brian, to solve the mystery. Was Amos King murdered because of the quilt? Who broke into the country store? It was time for Sammy and Brian to unmask the intruder. $4.95

#2   **Bird in the Hand** by Ken Munro
When arson is suspected on an Amish farm, the village of Bird-in-Hand responds with a fund-raiser. The appearance of a mysterious tattooed man starts a series of events that ends in murder. And who is The Bird? Only Bird-in-Hand's own teenage detectives can unravel the mystery. $5.95

#3   **Amish Justice** by Ken Munro
The duo turns into a trio when Joyce Myers becomes the newest member of the Sammy and Brian detective team. Is farmland in Lancaster County worth killing for? Frank Crawford thinks so. And when the police call the attempts on his life accidents, the old farmer sends for the teenage detectives. The three sleuths soon discover one of five suspects knows about the "IT" under the house. $5.95

#4   **Jonathan's Journal** $5.95
Buy them at your local bookstore or use this convenient coupon for ordering.

I am enclosing $_____ (please add $2.00 for postage and handling). Send check or money order only.

Name _____

Address _____

City _____ State _____ Zip Code _____